The Derbyshire Set – Book 2

Regency Historical Romance

The Captains

Compromised Heiress

Arietta Richmond

Dreamstone Publishing © 2015

www.dreamstonepublishing.com

ISBN: 1925165612

ISBN-13:   978-1-925165-61-6

Books by Arietta Richmond

The Derbyshire Set

The Earl's Unexpected Bride

The Captain's Compromised Heiress

The Viscount's Unsuitable Affair

The Count's Impetuous Seduction

The Rake's Unlikely Redemption

The Marquess' Scandalous Mistress

Stand-alone novel

The Scottish Governess

The Crew of the Seadragon's Soul Series, coming soon

A set of 10 linked novels

Dedication

For everyone who had the grace to be patient while this book, and the ones before and after it, were coming into existence, who provided cups of tea, and food, when the writing would not let me go, and endured countless times being asked for opinions. And for all the writers of Regency Historical Romance, whose books I read, who inspired me to write in this fascinating period.

Chapter One

The moment that Lady Blanchette saw Captain Westbury's uniform, she knew that this party had not been a mistake. For days now she had argued with her mother and sister, insisting that it was all too soon, too close to the nightmare that had been her aborted wedding to the Earl of Stanningfield, for her to be able to cope with society once again. They had recited the same old arguments; she needed to move ahead in her life, she couldn't go on moping and crying, over having been jilted at the altar, for ever more.

The incident may have stirred up a scandal in Derbyshire society and beyond, but she was still one of the most desirable young ladies in England, with a substantial portion as well, and would surely find a suitable match soon enough. She had dismissed all of their reasoning and sulked, but, in that instant of her first sight of Captain Westbury, with her heart pitter-pattering like a cantering mare, all that could be put aside.

Hope, romance, and desire all rose suddenly within her, fresh sensations once again.

'Captain Henry Westbury of the Coldstream Guards, heir to The Most Honourable Sir Thomas Westbury, Marquess of Bevington.' The footman, in his sumptuous livery, made the announcement over the sound of the room's chatter, and it took an immense effort for all of the ladies present to maintain their calm demeanour and resist the urge to turn, as one, and stare at this new arrival.

His rank and title spoke for him - a soldier, so gallant and well-attired, and also with a claim to one of the great estates in England. Such a man would be a desirable husband for any daughter of a noble family, and all present were immediately aware of that fact. Not only this however, but from the perspective of a young lady, with ideas about romance learned from novels and whispered gossip between sisters, this Captain Westbury was an exceptionally handsome gentleman.

His golden hair sat thick and lush upon his head, immaculately curled, matching the colour of his shining brass buttons. The military stock and collar, in the dark facings of his most esteemed regiment of guardsmen, seemed almost to frame his face like a painting, and perfectly emphasised the delicate curvature of his bone structure, slender and pleasing. There was serenity in his blue eyes that nevertheless, when matched with his glorious mane and shimmering scarlet uniform seemed to give him an inner strength that radiated outwards. He was tall and well-proportioned, with long-legs clad in skin-tight buff breeches and high leather boots, designed for the parade ground and polished to a glinting sheen.

His entire manner and bearing was confident, even heroic, and he strode out into the room with every female eye fixed discreetly, or not so discreetly, upon him.

Blanche suppressed an urge to laugh. Could it really have been only a few hours ago that she had been sitting in the library of this very house, her house, here on the edge of Amfield Moor, morosely carrying on a conversation with her sister Charlotte about her desire to run away and be done with men and society for good?

'Oh Blanche, you must not talk such rubbish!' Charlotte had declared back confidently.

'Why just because one eligible bachelor has spurned you does not mean that they all will! What happened in Suffolk was a freak, a bizarre little incident that historians will look at a hundred years from now and declare to be one of the strangest occurrences in the annals of the English gentry! You were just unlucky that's all'.

'But Charlotte...' Blanche had replied, trying with all her might not to burst into tears once again. '... What if it's me? What if there is something about me, which Stanningfield, Charles, found profoundly unattractive? What if it's all somehow my problem and men don't take to me?'

'My dear Blanche, I am not sure what that is even supposed to mean. Why, you're pretty, you're clever, you're from an exceptionally good family, if I do say so myself. Don't talk rubbish! If you are to declare that you have certain deficiencies of appearance or character that make you unattractive, what possible hope is there for me?'

They had shared a little laugh at this. It had always been known to both of them that Blanche was, as the eldest and the prettier of the pair, the one who would be first to find a husband.

She secretly suspected that Charlotte resented her for this fact, but her sister was kind and knowing enough not to let on. The truth was that Blanche's failed marriage put Charlotte in a very awkward position. It was unlikely that a betrothal would be sought, or agree if proposed for he, until her older sister was herself wed.

Indeed, in her worst moments, Charlotte did wonder if, as the youngest, there was a chance that her family might decide they would rather not be parted from her ever, if she did not have the chance to seek a husband soon. An unsaid tension was growing between the two sisters, despite Charlotte's willingness to try and stem her sisters' tears.

'Here is my personal guarantee' Charlotte had declared, smiling. 'If you don't have attractive and suitable gentlemen positively queueing up to ask you to dance with them at the ball tonight, why then I'll personally ride naked through the streets of Chesterfield. You have that as a guarantee, signed by my own hand and sealed with the Cavendish family crest!' Blanche was rather shocked by that image, but had laughed nonetheless. They had shaken hands in a comical imitation of City gentlemen, and embraced.

The truth from Blanche's perspective was that she had never doubted Charlotte's prospects of finding a man. She could be very funny and was shamelessly flirtatious, and their mother had never suggested keeping either of them unwed.

Perhaps the younger of the Cavendish sisters knew that having a moping spinster ahead of her in the marriage queue was no good to anyone. Whatever her motives, Blanche was glad of the kindness. Now that Captain Westbury had made his appearance she was more than glad.

In fact, she was positively delighted that her mother had decided to host this house party, and ball (the fact that it allowed her mother to indulge in her penchant for bringing together unwed persons of distinction was a side benefit, from Blanche's point of view), and that so many had decided to come. None had yet raised the subject of her unfortunate jilting at the hands of Charles Rockingham, Earl of Stanningfield, many of whom present privately knew to be an eccentric and impulsive sort of a man in any case.

For a while she had sat at the back of the room gathering her courage and resolve, sipping at a glass of ratafia, while Charlotte batted her eyelashes and laughed at the men's jokes, but now she pressed forward, concealing half of her beautiful heart shaped face with a fan, and casting what she hoped were dark and mysterious looks with her piercing gaze. She could see immediately that Captain Westbury, who was still by the door exchanging pleasantries with his hosts, her mother and father, had noticed her.

She was not in the least surprised when he ignored several of the ladies nearer the entrance, blushing and fiddling with their hair, and made straight for her. The newfound sense of confidence, that this created, carried her into their conversation with a strong sense of her attractiveness, and of the ample possibilities this evening, and the rest of this week, afforded.

'Lady Blanchette, I assume?' he asked wryly, bending to kiss her hand in a single, practised motion. Her heart fluttered and she felt something new stirring in her, low in her body. It was a sensation she was quite unused to, a trembling and a warmth. She had felt desire before, had felt nervous, had felt many things, but never exactly this.

It startled her, but, if pressed, she would not have said that it was an unpleasant sensation. She looked at Captain Westbury's clean-cut jawline, and felt his firm hand around hers and the sensation came on all the stronger.

'You presume correctly, Captain Westbury' she replied, barely making eye contact. She could see that Charlotte, on the other side of the room, had noticed and was now watching, distracted, no longer all that interested in the red-haired fellow she had been flirting with.

'Tell me, what brings a soldier of the esteemed Coldstream Guards to our humble occasion at Amfield?'

'Why, the same things that attract anyone to an occasion such as this - the promise of society with one's peers, of hunting, and the prospect of meeting, and conversing with, attractive young ladies.'

'And I trust your hopes in that regard have not been disappointed?'

'Certainly not.' He had a direct and bluff manner of speaking that she suspected he had learned in the military. 'I had heard about his Lordship's fair young daughters and assumed that reports of their grace and beauty had been exaggerated.

But now that I am able to make a reconnaissance with my own eyes, I can see that they were quite understated in their praise'.

'You think so? And may I hope that it is not daughters in the plural that you are here to make an aesthetic appraisal of?'

For the first time she allowed herself to make full eye contact with him. Their eyes met, two pools of intense blue, each hinting at fascinating hidden depths. He seemed momentarily taken off guard by her quip, and her heart picked up its pace once again, at precisely the same moment that the string quartet on the far side of the room increased their tempo. Was it the music, she thought for a second, that was making her feel like this, or the company?

'I shall have to see.' He responded coolly. 'After all, it would be ill-mannered of me not to make the effort of acquainting myself with all of the young ladies present, would it not?'

'I suppose that depends on your perspective' she said, with a flutter of her fan.

'Nevertheless' he said, regaining some composure, 'I was considering asking you to dance with me at once, and I would consider it most disappointing if you were to refuse. May I dare to hope that there may be a space on your dance card – for this very dance?'

Blanche made show of consulting her dance card carefully, even though she knew exactly what was written on there – which was, due to her hiding in shadows earlier, precisely nothing. She looked up, and was immediately caught again by his deep blue eyes.

'Would you be so very disappointed Captain? I suppose in that case, I should feel duty-bound to accept.'

With an intriguing smile, that promised much but gave away almost nothing, she placed her hand daintily on his offered arm, and allowed him to take her off to the centre of the room to dance.

The Right Honourable James Blackwood was a lot more than just the heir of the Viscount Selby. Aside from his title, he had rather a reputation, some of which was hard-won, but some of which never seemed to stop chasing him. He was renowned as one of the best shots in the kingdom, having brought down a reputed two score and a dozen grouse on the Glorious Tenth three years ago. He was also a superb huntsman, a fine addition to any party, hard-riding and with a talent for scenting a fox.

All admirable traits. But, unfortunately, perhaps, in addition to these he was a gambler, a drinker, and a notorious rake. He hosted parties at his house in Nottinghamshire which were known to go on for days and days of rowdy cavorting – the sort of parties where the ladies present were certainly not of the nobility. He was friends with strange and dangerous men; poets, painters, Italians and Turks, and had travelled far and wide.

Some said that he had killed a man in Greece for bringing him the wrong vintage of wine. Some had said he had seduced the Mistress of the King of Prussia, and been banished from that kingdom for ever. It was even said, in a few especially sensational whispers, that he had fathered the present dauphin of France in an especially daring and violent affair before the conclusion of the wars with Napoleon. Whether there was any truth to any of this was impossible to establish for certain, and Blackwood himself never deigned to comment.

What was undeniably true, and what formed the basis for much of this reputation, was that Blackwood was one of the most skilful seducers in England. There was a trail of conquests behind him, and many of them had let the world know about his skills. He was good-looking, but not exceptionally so. There was an edge of darkness and danger to his appearance, from his jet black hair and cynical eyes, to the shadows that seemed to cling to his jawline and the easy way in which he raised his left eyebrow, as a comment, in itself, on the conversation.

His lip seemed to form a permanent slightly sardonic half smile that was, apparently, still beguiling to the ladies, and he rarely raised a true smile, even at the best efforts of ladies and gentlemen alike to stimulate his sense of humour. His voice had a resonant, rasping tone that came from his years of hard-living, and from the musky cigarillos, which he imported directly from the West Indies, and smoked with frequency. Young ladies often flinched from him at first, but they soon found that what they first experienced as a sort of dread quickly turned into fascination, and then passionate attraction. Blackwood knew the effect that he had on people and he knew how to use it to get what he desired.

When James Blackwood heard that Lady Blanchette Cavendish had been abandoned at the altar by Stanningfield, a former companion of his, his interest was piqued. Lady Blanchette was an intensely pretty girl and he had made her acquaintance some years ago. She was already betrothed then, but he had still done all that he could to ingratiate himself, inviting her fascination, coaxing her to laugh at his remarks even when they were not all that amusing, leaving confident that she would think of him more, and even allow his image to stray into the realm of her fantasies.

He considered her very attractive even by his own high standards, the equal at least of many of the ladies in the courts of Europe that he had visited in his time. It amused him, in a somewhat twisted way, to be able to draw the affections even of ladies promised to another, especially to someone like Stanningfield, with whom he was no longer on such good terms. So when the invitation to a week-long house party and ball at Amfield House had arrived, he had been pleased. He had suspected at once that Blanchette would not only be present but in a fragile state, still mourning the loss of her promised husband, shaken by her embarrassment in front of society, and most likely receptive to the advances of an attractive and well-bred bachelor, whom she had already met. He estimated that most of the other gentlemen there would be young, inexperienced, a little over-enthusiastic and unpolished in the art of seduction, looking to start a serious affair rather than a pleasurable liaison.

He would therefore stand out in the room, due to his reputation and his manners, and he knew for a fact that Amfield House was plenty big enough to accommodate the fruition of a seduction.

Anticipation had roused his manhood to turgidity, and he had set out for the ball, attended by his loyal valet, Buckham, and with late night pleasure on his mind.

'The Right Honourable James Blackwood, heir to the Viscount Selby.'

There was an almost audible gasp in response to the announcement of his arrival. He was wearing his best black dress coat, and his cravat tied in the manner most fashionable in London society. He glanced casually around the room, immediately taking command of his surroundings. Young ladies looked at him in awestruck fascination and gentlemen with instinctive unease. A number of the younger gentlemen present immediately made very unsubtle defensive shifts to shield their sweethearts from his sight, and potential attentions.

Blackwood almost laughed. He was well used to this. Soon enough they would be slapping him on the back and boasting to him about their hunting prowess, trying as hard as they could to ingratiate themselves with this notorious dandy before he ingratiated himself with the women they desired. For now though, their reaction at hearing his name was one of mild panic.

The only people in the room who did not seem scandalised at his appearance were his hosts, the Earl and Countess Derbyshire, but then they were rather older than most of those present in the room (save the well-attired chaperones who sat around the fringe looking mildly bored), and did not move in circles where the principle conversation was salacious gossip.

They had always considered Blackwood to be rather charming, and greeted him now with a warmth and grace he rarely received elsewhere.

'Ah, James!' declared Lady Derbyshire, beaming. She was a large woman in every conceivable sense, taller and heftier than her husband, with a booming voice and open manners for a lady of her station.

'So excellent of you to come, I had feared an occasion such as this might prove a little drab for an experienced and well-socialised fellow such as yourself!'

'Not at all, My Lady.'

Blackwood smiled, kissing her hand politely as she offered it.

'There is little on this good earth I value more than a good house party and ball at Amfield House, with persons of quality. The hunting here is always excellent. Regarding the room, I can see that you have excelled yourselves once more.'

'I see you have not lost your powers of flattery!' said Lord Derbyshire, shaking his hand firmly. 'I should hope that you do not employ them on the delicate sensibilities of the young ladies present, my dear Blackwood!'

'Indeed not, My Lord.' Blackwood replied promptly 'My wild oats are quite sown, your guests need not fear my bachelor's status. I fear that, as the heir to a humble estate, I am used to certain habits of ingratiation as a necessary function of my society...'

'You are as modest as you ever were!' said Lady Derbyshire, casting him a wry glance.

'Now you must excuse me' Blackwood said to his hosts, privately keen to move beyond these formalities. '- I shall now avail myself of your no doubt excellent punch, and make my salutations to your charming daughters.'

'Well we would not wish to deprive them of your excellent company, Blackwood', chortled Lord Derbyshire, blinded to the intentions of his guest. 'We shall attend to greeting the rest of our guests. I believe young Blanchette is already developing a fondness for a young officer of the guards, see over there?'

Blackwood followed the line of his finger to Blanchette, and their eyes met. She was indeed dancing with a young, blonde fellow in a soldier's uniform. He sensed a mild shock in her as she noticed his presence, as if she were immediately distracted and unsure what to think.

'Best break 'em up before anything unseemly breaks out, eh?' said Lord Derbyshire, with a wink.

Blackwood smiled in acknowledgement of his host's saucy joke, and, as the music came to a conclusion, and the dancers left the floor, started his move across the room.

'You will forgive me my sudden interjection...' he said in his husky tone. The pair, who had been moving to the refreshments table, turned to face him. The officer, whom he observed, with a tiny note of regret, was a terribly handsome young fellow - and taller than he was – looked somewhat taken aback. Blanchette however, looked immediately delighted. A spectacular smile quickly spread across her face.

'Mr. Blackwood!' she exclaimed in delight. 'Why it's been such a long while since we have seen you! So good of you to have come!'

'You look absolutely divine' he said at once, wearing his easy confidence lightly. He reached for her, sliding his fingers over the sensitive skin of her palm in a caress that was effective even through gloves, and unseen by anyone else, as he bent kiss her hand. He looked up and saw that she was looking right at him, the pupils of her shimmering blue eyes dilated slightly. He could already sense that their attraction was mutual. 'It is quite worth the ride up from Nottinghamshire, just to see you again. It was so good of you to invite me.'

'Not at all! You were certainly atop my proposed guest list.'

'You are too kind. As you are well aware, occasions such as this have a tendency to bring out the absolute worst in me' they held each other's gaze as Blanche giggled lightly. His touch was already working.

'But then we wouldn't want a boring and tiresome ball now, would we? Or a tiresome week, for that matter – hunting only goes so far for amusement.'

'Why no, sir. Most emphatically not – I have been quite bored enough in my life.'

'I am sorry.' Captain Westbury cut in assertively. His interruption disrupted a moment of dark excitement, of quivering attraction growing in Blanchette's bosom. She turned, and for a moment it was he who had the lady's attention. He went to place his hand on her shoulder but she shifted instinctively to the right to avoid it.

Instead, he stepped forward to place his powerful military frame between Blanchette and this dark and, to him, somewhat ominous looking intruder.

15

'I do not believe we have been introduced, Mr...?' he said the 'mister' disdainfully, placing stress on Blackwood's lack of estate or title.

If only, Blackwood had often thought to himself on occasions such as this, my old uncle Selby would do the decent thing and be deceased, and let me inherit his Viscountcy!

'Blackwood.'

'Pleased to meet you sir, I am Captain Henry Westbury of the Coldstream Guards.' He spoke with the rat-a-tat tone and graceless clarity of the officer's mess.

'Charmed' said Blackwood ironically. 'It is pleasing to see that we have a trained warrior in our midst. Should Bonaparte escape from St. Helena and deign to invade Amfield Moor I am sure we shall be quite safe with you around.'

Westbury, rather shocked at the disrespect implied, made to stutter a reply but could not think of anything. 'Aha!' thought Blackwood. 'This bounder might have the looks and rank, but I've got all the wit!'

'Now excuse us, I fear we may be occupying a little too much room on the dance floor, we'd best retire to the fringes. I trust you shall enjoy the remainder of your evening, Captain Westbury.' Blackwood threw Westbury a cruel glance, and led Blanchette, who already seemed to be under his spell, away from her handsome Guardsman.

'So what can you tell me of the French ladies, Mr. Blackwood?'

'Well, they are certainly fair, and very fashionable. So many of them have a worldly sort of air about them, as if nothing you could do could possibly impress them. They are far more assertive than the English girls as well. In France, it is very often they who lead the gentlemen, and not the other way around.'

'Heavens!' said Blanchette, fascinated by Blackwood's experiences. 'I cannot even imagine such a situation!'

'Nor could I until I went there, but I am compelled to report that many of the things one hears about the ways of French ladies are true. They are not however, my specialist subject. Until the conclusion of the war of course, France and its manifold delights were quite closed off to us.'

'And with good reason!' Blanchette cut in. 'Bonaparte had designs on the whole of Europe!'

'I suppose that all depends on your point of view' said Blackwood, casting his troubled glance into the middle distance. 'Politics has always bored me terribly. I have often thought it would be best if all the governments of the world would simply abandon their little schemes for the dominance of one another and let those of us who appreciate life more live as we pleased. The Italians understand that, for example...'

'That is most unpatriotic of you, Mr. Blackwood!'

'Perhaps it is' he said casually. Blanchette was quite scandalised but she could not shut off her ears or eyes from the intriguing observations and opinions of this man. The very fact that he felt at liberty to make her feel scandalized caused a delicious shiver to run down her spine. His was quite the most dangerous company she had ever kept, and that excited her more than it should. It was as if, in his company, none of the usual rigid formality and expectation of society seemed to apply, and one could simply say whatever one wanted. Or for that matter, do whatever one wanted...

'...but I have always found that the Italians appear to have their priorities set right. We English, and others of the northern nations on the continent, are so uptight, so proper, so concerned with our little plans and designs, with commerce and politics.'

'And it is right that we should be so!' chuckled Blanchette, aware that she was playing devil's advocate.

She had seen none of the world beyond England's shores and could only guess at what it was like from what she heard from men like Blackwood. It was entirely possible that his opinions were correct. 'Through our industry and our unparalleled constitution, we have come to rule half the world!'

'… and if that is what concerns you, Lady Blanchette, then that is all well and good. However, I am interested in more than money and colonies. I am interested in the heart and soul of man, and indeed…' he leaned closer to her and placed his strong hand on hers discreetly. There were no chaperones nearby to chastise him, and Blanche's mother and father were, again, distracted by new arrivals at the door.

A small part of Blanchette was fearful of this rogue, who had sailed the seven seas, but most of her was glad that no-one was looking on. Her heart thundered beneath her stays and her womanhood prickled with heat. She felt as if she had never been so excited – was this, she wondered, what they meant when they spoke of lust ? Did she desire this man, in a carnal way ? She had felt desire before, of that nature, though she would not admit it to anyone, but it had never felt like this.

'… the heart and soul of woman, as well.' Blackwood almost whispered in her ear. She held fast against his proximity, if only because if she leaned any closer to him in turn they would soon be atop one another. Not that, at this moment, she would mind being hard up against his strong body, but…. There were too many people around them, who might, at any moment, turn and see, such a thing was unthinkable, here. Well perhaps not unthinkable… but certainly not acceptable!

'Pray tell Mr. Blackwood...' she said, feigning innocence. 'How do the fairest ladies of Derbyshire County compare to those of say, Italy, or France?' She leant forward, and wriggled away from his disturbing touch, if only temporarily.

Then she looked him straight in the eye, for a lingering moment that said more than any words ever could.

'How do we measure up?'

'Well-' he replied, with a whimsical little smile '- all company is mixed, of course, it is rare in heaven or earth to find a room filled exclusively with young ladies whose prettiness is beyond question. But I would have to say that the best amongst present company...' he looked at her again, steely and wry, a glint of something hungry in his dark eyes, as if in his mind he was already tearing off her bodice and hitching up her petticoats. She didn't allow him to hold her gaze, and instead cast a glance off to the left, where she assumed Captain Westbury would be skulking around feeling thwarted.

'... would be a match for any of the greatest beauties of the world.' Blanchette's stomach did a little tumble. She could feel the hairs on her arm prickling, standing to attention. Her hand strayed down to brace her against the back of a chair next to where they stood, her legs were suddenly shaky, and it seemed that a lightning bolt ran through her as his hand brushed her elbow. She was hot and felt strangely warm and damp between her legs, all for him, for this dark and handsome traveller, this seducer, this knave. Just from a short conversation, and a light brushing touch – what was happening to her?

She was a well-bred young lady, she should not be thinking like this, and she should certainly not be enjoying it!

Yet... she knew that she was capable of enjoying this, for she had explored that possibility before... she shut those thoughts down. She was not going to remember, to even consider, such things.

Yet the temptation was too great – she had spent so long expecting to marry Charles, yet she had never felt this level of excitement with him. No, whispered an insidious little voice in her mind, you have only ever felt anything like this with the man beside you now, and, for a moment earlier, with Captain Westbury....

Blanche made a sudden decision – tonight, she would be brave, would act on her own desires, regardless of what a well-bred young lady "should do", and would leave dealing with any consequences for tomorrow. With her past, surely nothing she chose to do would make her any worse off!

'Mr. Blackwood,' she said in her best impression of a plain and simple maiden 'I would be most honoured if you would accompany me to the library. We have a fine selection of volumes about various parts of the world, I would be interested in your opinion of their veracity...' she turned her head slightly to the right, watching his reaction from the corner of her eye. She could not help but notice his open gait, the strength of his posture, and the proximity of his body to hers. His beautifully tailored tight fitting breeches displayed his body to perfection, and left her in little doubt that he desired her.

21

'... and we also have a globe, and certain other accoutrements that I would be willing to show you.'

'That sounds most interesting, my Lady' he purred back. 'Lead on'.

The library at Amfield House was indeed impressive. It was well respected among the great families of central England for its elegant design and superb collection of volumes. High cases of shelves ran all around the perimeter from floor to ceiling, and some of the books were only accessible by ascending a ladder.

There were several sets of tables and chairs, all varnished to a sheen and beautifully upholstered, scattered about the room, with small piles of books upon them. A few larger couches were placed to one side. A cabinet of exotic curiosities, acquired by the Cavendish family over the years, sat in one corner, including a shrunken head from the Americas and a great claw, from an unknown creature, which some obscure relative had picked up in the South Seas.

At the back of the room, by a high window, was an escritoire, and on it, a great globe made at some point in the last century to commemorate the discovery of Australia.

'You have a very fine library' said Mr. Blackwood on entering, casually closing and locking the door. He walked across the room, regarding Blanchette from behind with a heated stare that she could not see. She was shapely, and had always appealed to him, and their conversation so far had brought him to a pitch of lust that he had not felt for some time.

He supposed that it was the possibility of debauching such a delectable innocent, with her cooperation. At least he assumed that she was innocent – he wondered if Stanningfield had had the balls to take advantage of his betrothed, before he jilted her at the altar.

'I would certainly be interested in making an appraisal of your collections...' Blanche had stopped near the globe and, as he stepped up behind her, firmly repressing his desire to immediately fondle her easily reachable buttocks, she turned, and before he could utter any more inane formal conversation, Blanche had grabbed him, and was kissing him, inexpertly, but with feverish enthusiasm.

She was not entirely sure what had come over her, and knew that this was a most improper way to behave, even within the bounds of the 'unwritten code of possible improper behaviour' for unmarried ladies. Whilst she had certainly carried out some extensive 'exploration' with Charles, she had always waited for him to initiate it, and had been somewhat disappointed by the whole thing.

After the weeks of depression and tears since her aborted wedding to Charles, the effect of being so obviously desired acted like an aphrodisiac flowing through her, through her lips and tongue, her newly found courage fuelled by desire of her own.

Blackwood, though surprised for a moment, quickly regained his composure and took charge of the kiss, applying all of his expertise to deepening it, and taking full advantage of her enthusiasm.

They collapsed onto the nearby, large, well stuffed leather couch together, bound at the mouth.

Slowly, without forcing the issue or making her feel uncomfortable, he began to run his firm, strong hands all over her delicate body, careful not to scare her – he wanted her, he was so hard that it hurt, but he would take his time about it – these things were to be savoured, at least the first time, with such a woman. Silently and smoothly he began to undo the tiny buttons at the back of her gown, then to loosen the laces of her stays, gently easing the gown off her shoulders, and kissing his way down her neck and onto the delectable top slope of her breasts.

Easing the fabric down further, his kisses following its path, he reached to ease her beautiful breasts up and out of the corset, just enough to reach her nipples. Blanche was lost in the sensations, her breathing was fast and shallow, and her body seemed not her own. It was as if she was someone completely different, some daring woman who knew what she was doing, knew what she wanted, and was not afraid at all.

Blackwood's tongue reached one nipple as his clever fingers found the other, and, as he caressed her breasts with an amazing contrast of warm mouth and lightly pinching fingers, she felt another jolt, as if she had been suddenly struck by some force inside her, and found that there were muscles clenching inside her, in response – muscles that she had never, prior to this day, suspected to exist.

She clung to him tightly, and though still almost fully clothed they seemed to be pressing into each other's bodies through the layers of cloth and undergarments.

'You are a most spirited girl Lady Blanchette.' His voice was husky, his breathing heavy, as she indulged her newly aroused appetite for kissing and exploration with kisses to his cheek and neck.

'Do you treat all of your gentleman admirers in this unorthodox fashion?' she drifted another kiss across the stubble on his jawline, and looked up at him as he leaned in closer to her. In an instant he was kissing her again. She returned the kiss enthusiastically, pressing her body against him, as he ran his hand down over her hip, feeling her delightful shape, through the all too many layers of the fabric of her skirts, until he reached the hem, and could slide his hand up again, drawing those skirts with it.

'Only those whom I deem worthy of my affections, Mr. Blackwood.'

Her reply came on little gasping breaths as his fingers slid up the silken skin of her inner thigh, and then across the fabric of her drawers towards her most intimate place.

She arched her body up against him, and he bent to lick and suck at her nipples again, one then the other, as his fingers worked gently and insistently under her skirts. There was much, much too much fabric still between them – he most strongly wished that he could see her body laid bare, but that would have to wait for another time.

He was deservedly proud of his skills in the sensual arts, of his understanding of what women enjoyed most – after all, he had spent years perfecting that knowledge.

It was a simple matter to ensure that what he did was having a deeply exciting effect on her.

Blanche was arching her hips and moving herself against his hand, tossing her head from side to side, moaning quietly, as he built the intensity of sensation, working her nub of pleasure mercilessly with his fingers. She quivered out a sigh and looked at him with eyes glazed with need.

'And tell me...' he added, pressing his brow against hers, breathing the words against her lips, whilst his finger never stopped in their work '... was Charles Rockingham considered suitable for such attentions?'

For a second, even deep in desire as she was, she was quite taken aback at his cheek. To raise the subject of her recent betrothal in her very own house! It was all rather too much to take in, all too shocking. But, as his fingers continued their work, and her body responded, regardless of her thoughts, she realised the purpose of his remark. He was asking after the state of her virginity. Just as he had coaxed these untamed passions out of her, so too was he forcing an admission of another sort.

'We did, commune, in a nature such as this, on more than one occasion.' She said it without either guilt or shame, even though she knew that society would say that she would feel both. She knew that she need not expect judgement from a man like James Blackwood.

'Very well. I do not make a habit of robbing un-betrothed ladies of their innocence. You may call it one of the few genuine principles I hold. But it seems, as you have already been quite stripped of all innocence, that I may proceed free of guilt.'

He did not say the rest of his thought, which was to the effect that he felt sure that he was capable of teaching her far more 'uninnocent' things than Stanningfield would ever have done.

She could not stop herself from laughing, and then kissing him once again, almost frantically. What a rare intrusion of honour into the conduct of Mr. Blackwood! His concern for her future prospects of marriage was quite admirable, and she could not help but feel all the greater affection for him.

After all, her current state of 'lack of innocence' was all her own fault, but at least here and now she could enjoy the results.

She pushed aside any thought of how she might deal with an eventual explanation to a husband, should there ever be one.

That was a problem that already existed, and what she did here today would not change that. Blackwood's fingers had not stopped their work, and her need was intense now, and seemed more important than anything else.

Blackwood abandoned conversation, his lust having risen to a fever pitch upon realizing that he could take her now, with no impediment, and have the pleasure, as well, of showing up Stanningfield as a poor lover, in the process. He began kissing her again, working his way downwards, from her lips which he kissed passionately, putting all of his well-practised sensuality into it, back to her delicious breasts.

He pulled her bodice further aside in what seemed to be single, clean movement and lifted her breasts further from the corset, fully exposing her pink nipples to his rampant tongue again.

All the while he continued to work his fingers ever deeper into her underclothes, until they slid through the slit in her drawers to touch her wet folds directly.

She writhed momentarily with pleasure at this instant of contact. He licked and lapped little circles around her sensitive breasts, drawing gasps and sighs of pleasure, and a growing shaking all through, all down to her dripping wet womanhood.

Any thoughts of resistance, or of pulling out of this mad, sudden seduction, which rose in Blanche's mind, were immediately suppressed. She had no desire to be anywhere but here, doing this, with this man, right now. Her nipples hardened further and seemed almost to push outwards from her body, her breasts newly swollen by desire.

Though she had expected it, the sensation of his fingers direct on her most sensitive flesh was not in any way dimmed by that expectation, indeed it was all the more electrifying for the build-up that had gone before.

His fingers continued to rub away in the same dextrous manner that they had worked when touching her through her clothes, moving over all of her womanhood, in ways that Charles had never touched her, and stimulating her further with every caress.

Shockwaves ran through her, emanating out from the point of his touch, and she could feel the wet desire pouring out of her as he increased the tempo of his motions. They continued to kiss, nipping at each other's lips with their teeth. She almost hissed back at him like a cat, but instead she lay back further on the chair and let her desire overrule everything, allowing him to do as he wished, revelling in the sensations which rushed through her body.

Leaving off his attention to her breasts, Blackwood worked his way under her skirts. For a second she wondered what on earth he was doing, but before she knew it she could feel it well enough. His tongue, muscular and well-practised, was pressing against her nub of pleasure, at first lightly, in gentle, rhythmical laps, but then with greater speed and intensity.

He started languidly, licking at her entire region with slow, deep tongue motions, but then began to concentrate his efforts on the one, most sensitive part, the heavenly dimple that sat just above the rest of it. He enclosed it in his whole mouth and with his tongue still working, pistoning away, he sucked hard and drew gasps of pleasure from her. She was quite overcome by physical sensation, all thoughts seemed to drift into the ether, and she forgot even who and where she was. This pleasure was all that there was. A huge wave of pleasure crashed through her, and she lay back, dazed.

Before she realised that he had moved, her lover had re-emerged into the light, and then she was kissing him once again, passionate kisses, expressing her gratitude for the pleasure that he had just given her. He allowed her a brief pause to collect herself, holding her in a powerful embrace that send warm shivers all through her. Then he was back to attend to her, not with his tongue or finger this time, but with his breeches about his knees, exposing his well-travelled thighs and firm buttocks to the air, his large cock hard and forward-facing, ready to deliver pleasure for himself, as well as for her.

He had not been this hard, or enjoyed himself this much for some time – there was a lot to be said for debauching supposedly innocent daughters of the nobility, rather than world weary widows and prostitutes.

Softly, he slid himself in, and she could feel herself glistening with wet readiness for his thrust, anticipation of the pleasure to come forming like a pool around her loins.

He pressed forward and she pulled him in with a lingering sigh, mellow but promising of so much more, of moans and screams of pleasure ready to burst from her lips, should he choose to cause them.

Blackwood savoured the sensation – she was deliciously tight around him, and oh, so responsive.

Blanche floated in the sensations, unable to prevent herself from comparing this to her previous exploration of intimate relations with Charles. Unlike her only previous lover, Blackwood did not seek to pin her down or impose himself almost violently. His approach was so much more refined and practised!

Where Charles had seemed desperate, and hurried, Blackwood seemed almost to anticipate her sensations, appreciate her needs, and allow her space in which to feel and experience all of this. She was wide open with delight.

In one smooth and controlled motion he began to move. His entire body swayed with a singular rhythm, a pulse flowing through him and into her, undulating, gyrating, stimulating her in exactly the right place and sending sensations crackling up her all the way to the top of her head.

Her nipples were sensitive, unbelievably hard and extended out, towards her lover, and her entire torso was consumed with the same feelings of warmth and light.

Never had she felt so brilliant, so utterly intoxicated with another human being, so attuned to her own body and to what it was capable of, what acute pleasures could be conjured from within and without. As if she was whole, quivering with delight, quaking here, in her parents' very own library, sensing that she could be anywhere on earth and not care, just as long as these pleasures were there as well.

He held himself closer to her, as close in fact, as it was physically possible for two people to be.

Their lips and tongues locked once again in the same sensual dance as before and she could feel every pulsation of his body, ever hammering blow of his heart, fused almost to hers through her breast and bodice.

He gasped 'my lady…' and all she could pant back was 'James… oh God, James…'

She wanted to say more, to articulate her appreciation, all the superlatives and positive words that seemed to assail her, but she could not, she was too overwhelmed to speak.

Words were inadequate for these feelings, some deeper and more powerful language had taken over. And then, with a sudden groan, almost of pain, and a swift motion that extracted him from her before dire consequences and bastard infants could be risked, it was over. Blackwood tumbled aside, wheezing his smoky breath into the carpet. Blanchette lay back on the couch and allowed herself to fade slowly back into the room.

'There' said Blackwood, smiling, as he stood and adjusted his clothes, restoring his usual immaculate appearance. '… that wasn't so bad, I trust? I hope that I have delivered an experience of better quality than those granted you previously?'

'No sir' she replied, hazily, rolling to her side on the couch. 'Not so very bad at all.' He planted a firm slap on her rump, and she felt suddenly a little shocked and disoriented.

'As I expected - all English girls are whores deep down!' he exclaimed, suddenly seeming to care not a bit for her or her wellbeing. Was all that care and attention that he had just shown her just to get his own pleasure, with no deeper feelings at all? She was, in that instant, filled with feelings of shame and regret. However great the pleasure that she had taken with him, his sudden apparent lack of care left her feeling somehow used, and a little dirty,

Was everything one heard about James Blackwood true then? Had she just made a terrible mistake in surrendering herself to him so fully? And what would he expect from her, over the week to come?

He pulled her to her feet, and, as he helped her restore her clothing to rights, looked at her dazed expression with amusement, and said 'Come on then Blanche', calling her by the private version of her first name, though he had no right to.

'Let's re-join the party.'

Back in the ballroom, Charlotte was having a more trying evening than she had hoped for. She had watched, impassive, as her sister had first been approached by the most handsome man present, Captain Westbury, and then been taken off, presumably to some terribly exciting mischief, by the most renowned seducer in the kingdom.

Despite the need for a well-bred young lady to keep up a composed and good-natured air on an occasion such as this, she could not help but breathe an audible sigh. It had ever been thus. All of the gentlemen's attentions were focussed on Blanche, the oldest, fairest, and most desirable of the two. Charlotte was left to trail in her older sister's wake.

It was not that she wished ill of Blanche, or that their relationship itself suffered unduly. They had been very close since they were small, and had always got on well.

Their nanny, Miss Partridge, had always remarked that whilst other infant ladies could be expected to tear each other's hair out the moment they were left unattended, you could leave the Cavendish sisters in the nursery alone together for hours on end, only to come back and find them putting the finishing touches to a redecorated doll's house, or reading quietly to one another. She had a lot of fondness for her sister which was perhaps rooted in their very different characters. While Charlotte was clever and funny, Blanche was the more thoughtful of the two, and had a quieter and more intense nature.

She could, of course, be outgoing, even assertive when she needed to be, but Charlotte suspected that it was in part her sisters' ability to listen and play the humble and shrinking young maiden that seemed to attract men to her more easily. It was a great regret of hers that the century did not seem quite ready for women who knew their own mind and expressed it freely. She, of course, did her best to get the most out of her time at the ball. She fluttered her fan and let her eyelashes tremble invitingly, keeping her smile to herself and waiting for men to draw it out of her. The form was easy enough to imitate, but the conversation did not seem to be going her way:

'And what pray, have you been reading sir, of late?' she had said to a boisterous son of a Marquess, a regular at her father's hunts.

'Reading?' he had barked back. His face was already ruddy from the punch, despite her mother's insistence that it be diluted.

'I could never stand books. Can't see any purpose to sticking your head in a book myself. Fills the brain with all sorts of peculiar notions, most unnatural. As my father always maintained, the only diversions fit for a young fellow are hunting, feasting and whoring, and not necessarily in that order!'

His friends, big, arrogant, hunting obsessed younger sons to a man, laughed along at this. One might even have slapped him on the back.

'But surely sir, one must tire of the same three amusements? Surely the feasting and the, as you might say, liaisons of the other sort, must make it harder to pursue a fox after a time?'

'I have never found that to be the case' he replied disinterestedly.

He had hoped that this pretty-faced lady would be easier conversational game than she had proved. She was mocking him, and he was just about clever enough to realise it. 'You are a strange girl, Miss Charlotte. Now if you'll excuse me...'

A little later, talking to another gentleman, fair-faced but a rather slow conversationalist, she knew immediately that she had gone too far in the telling of what she had hoped would be an amusing story:

'I'd heard that, on the first chase of the season, it is customary for the ladies of the estate to play amusing pranks on the gentlemen, for a little light amusement, you understand...' the man, sandy-haired and well-dressed, allowed his eye to drift into the middle distance.

Women were not generally expected, on occasions such as this, to tell lengthy anecdotes, certainly not in order to amuse the men.

'... so a number of years ago, when I was only fifteen, we took the entire custom to an unprecedented new level. The fellows were taking a quick dram before they mounted up, and they had all of them left their riding boots by the parlour door, not wanting to tramp all through the house in dirty leather, you see? Anyway, just as they were getting ready, we snuck in and put a good dollop of custard into each of their boots! At first we'd thought that they would notice at once and that it might deter them from heading out, but to our surprise, they went out all the same, custard-filled boots and all! Eventually the rigours of the ride forced some of it to come out of their boots and all up their breeches, even staining the flanks of the horses. A lot of them were very startled, his Lordship the Earl of Gloucester I believe was on the point of calling for his horse doctor to examine this strange yellow affliction. It was only when Mr. Danvers, renowned up and down the land for his tremendous appetites, deigned to taste the stuff that they ascertained that it was only custard! Oh, how we laughed!'

'Hmm' came the nonplussed reply.

'I can see why that might cause some amusement to a few silly girls, unused to the pleasures of the hunt. Nevertheless, I can personally see no humour whatsoever in disrupting those fellows' leisure like that. I strongly advise that you indulge in no further such japes again.'

The young man then managed to find some distant relatives on the other side of the room who he 'simply had to speak to'.

Charlotte was just beginning to despair of conversation, parties, and men altogether.

Try as she might, she could never seem to strike the right balance, or conform adequately to the expectations imposed on her by society's rigid rules and demands.

She was considering retiring early to her bed, but, at her mother's look of concern, she sighed, put on a cheerful face, and went looking for someone else to talk to.

Blanche and Mr. Blackwood were able to sneak back into the ballroom easily enough. Cautious of arousing suspicion, they promptly parted ways on re-entering the room, Blackwood to talk with a few fellows he was acquainted with, over by the punch bowl, Blanche to the other side of the room to find her sister. Who was deep in conversation with a bored looking matron (one of those invited to ensure that enough chaperones were present) - a conversation that it would be most impolite to interrupt.   Blanche felt a wash of disappointment, and paused, wondering what to do now.

Such feelings were almost immediately dispelled when she heard a slight but deliberate throat-clearing behind her. Turning, she was met by the still splendid sight of Captain Westbury, standing on his own and sipping at a glass of punch. Held offered a second glass to her, and she took it gratefully.

Despite his dazzling uniform, he had the air of a man who was a little deflated, and certainly did not appear to be enjoying himself.

'I was concerned that you had fled your own family's ball, Lady Blanchette.'

'Oh no, sir' she replied rapidly.

Had he sniffed her out, somehow? Could he tell that she had not five minutes before had her petticoats and bodice pulled aside? Could he smell James Blackwood on her breath and in her hair?

'I was merely taking in a little air, that is all.'

'I see, and in the company of Mr. Blackwood, I understand?'

'Yes, yes I was' she stammered nervously. The façade had been erected but it did not seem to be standing up very well.

'Well after all, it would not be proper for a young lady to be going off on her own, even at her own party, and he is a most respected gentleman.' Thoughts of their encounter raced through Blanche's mind, and it was all she could do not to bite her lip. What elemental forces of lust had come over her just before?

She kept up staring into Captain Westbury's startling blue eyes, which gave her the feeling that he could see right through her prevarication, hoping to throw him off her trail somehow.

'He is. Though I must confess, I have heard rather mixed reports as to the reputation of Mr. James Blackwood. Even in the army one hears of these sorts of things, you understand.'

'Yes, but I believe his character to be quite reformed. People tend to settle down and mellow out as they get older, don't they, even bachelors of his...' she paused to think. Words were not coming easily under this sort of concerted pressure '...type.'

'Perhaps' Westbury replied sagely, casting a glance over in the direction of Blackwood. His dark hair and jacket could be made out instantly, as if he had a special aura pulling fascination, suspicion, and the bodices of young ladies all at once towards him.

'One does hear of such things, also.'

He paused, and they turned to watch the couples dancing, noting one particularly energetic young lady, dancing with an obviously besotted gentleman.

'That young lady certainly appears to be enjoying herself.' He spoke almost wistfully, as if he envied the girl her happiness.

'Indeed she does, Captain Westbury', Blanche replied. 'It is a predilection of young ladies after all, to desire the attention of handsome gentlemen at balls.'

He looked at her, strong, stern, but with a little hint of humour and understanding curling the edge of his lip. *'The Captain is an attractive fellow'* she allowed herself to think, even in her post-Blackwood haze.

'Is it now?' he said drily. 'Once more, I must admit that even in the army we are aware of such matters. It would be ill-mannered, would it not, were I not now to renew my offer of a dance?'

'Some might consider it so. Alternatively, some might consider it a show of undue favour, should I grant you two dances at one ball.' Blanche's tone was flirtatious. 'Personally, I always aim to keep an open mind on questions of social custom and propriety.'

'Well then' he said, extending his arm to her 'I shall infer from that what I will, and offer you my hand.' With a subtle smile and a tiny fluttering deep inside her, where earlier she had been penetrated by another, she accepted his hand and stepped onto the floor with him, to join the waltz.

'Tell me a little of the army, Captain' Blanche said, as they swayed around the floor.

'Did you see any action, in the recent conflict?'

'I certainly did. I was in Portugal, as a young Lieutenant, and then at Waterloo.' Blanche trembled at the very sound of the latter word. Waterloo! That great and terrible battle that had taken place less than two years ago! She had heard so much about it, remembered the news flying through the provincial towns and villages, celebrated with bonfires and the pealing of bells. Her parents had hosted a banquet to toast Wellington's victory, and she had there seen grown men on the point of tears, so moved were they by patriotic feelings of gratitude.

And now she was here, dancing in the arms of a man who had been there, who had braved French musket shots and bayonets and come out of it intact.

What a remarkable occurrence this was. She looked up at his strong chin and chiselled jaw and could not help look at him with a new admiration, awe even. For a few moments, James Blackwood was quite forgotten.

'I have heard that Waterloo was quite a battle, Captain' she said, suppressing her interest and excitement. 'It must have been a most traumatic experience.'

'I suppose it was a little' he replied sternly. 'The strange truth though, is that one does get used to these things. After terrible things have happened around you sufficient times, you become numb to them. You merely brace yourself and do what needs to be done.'

They swayed firmly to the right. His arms now felt stronger, the torso she could feel beneath his beautiful uniform coat all the more muscle-bound and magnificent. She was not just dancing with any old soldier here, some boy from the officer's mess dressed up for battle, this was a real-life war hero, impassive and unflappable, stepping along with her, in her parents' very own ballroom.

A tingling ran up to her bosom from her most sensitive area, and she knew at once that she desired him.

'But enough talk of the campaign trail, it is not an easy subject for even an experienced soldier to consider. Indeed it is one that we would all prefer never to need to think about again. I am more interested in you, my Lady.' She turned her head upwards sharply to meet his gaze, and could not help but feel flattered at his interest.

She could happily have gone on all night asking him about his gallantry and derring-do on the battlefields on Europe, but then she supposed, it was probably rather different discussing such matters when one had actually been there, and seen the horror of it all up close.

'Pray tell, what does a young lady of breeding discuss with a fellow like James Blackwood?'

'All manner of things sir' she said at once, a little defensively. 'There are many topics of conversation to pursue. His travels for example, or our respective opinions on various significant subjects.'

'Yes, I suppose that should all be plain enough. I have heard that he is a well-travelled gentleman, certainly.'

'Indeed he is...' she glanced around the room, and saw Blackwood, looking slyly in their direction. She was too far away to really make it out, but she could have sworn that she saw him raise his eyebrow at her, in an ironic acknowledgement of her new dance partner.

'...not in the same manner as you, Captain Westbury, but he has journeyed across most of Europe nonetheless, and seen the interiors of great courts and palaces.'

'- and the interiors of many great ladies as well, no doubt...'

'Sir! I find that allusion to be most improper. That is slanderous and scandalous talk!'

'- and those of many not so great ladies as well, one suspects.' Westbury was not put off by her outrage.

He seemed determined to weed out her secrets, to force a confession. The rational part of her simply put it down to envy, but she could not help but feel that he was vocalising her own conscience, and the anxieties she herself had felt, before and after her encounter with Blackwood.

There seemed to be a sudden need to confide in this bluff and honourable soldier, even if his speech was more direct than she was used to.

No, no, no – that would not do at all, she most certainly could not confide her thoughts to him.

But what could she say? Perhaps just a little sharing of confidences would satisfy him?

'It would be dishonest of me to claim that he does not exert a certain effect upon a young lady, upon my very own self in fact...'

'What an intriguing reaction!' Westbury whispered to her, conspiratorially.

'I must say, Lady Blanchette, you have aroused my interest. It is not just for your beauty, wealth and title, you understand, you are a most fascinating girl by most other measures as well. It seems that you do not think about the world the same way as other young ladies of my acquaintance.'

His words evoked a strange feeling of hope in her. Perhaps.... perhaps this man could see her for more than her pretty face? She pressed herself closer to him, almost for comfort.

But where was he going with this? She desperately needed to turn his interest in her 'conversation' with Blackwood aside.

'You see, Captain Westbury, I have a confession to make...'

He looked at her, politely waiting for her to go on, although she could see that he would like to push her for more information, he did not.

'Mr Blackwood has been a friend of the family for some years - my parents are quite fond of him. I..... I ...' she hesitated, unsure of how to go on – she was telling the truth, but also, not all of it. 'A few years ago, as an impressionable young lady, I found him quite fascinating, and I fear that.... fascination.... has continued to exist, even through my betrothal to Charles.' She stuttered a little as she said it, and looked away, blushing, embarrassed.

He could not know that her blush was for her embarrassment at mentioning her aborted marriage, rather than her juvenile tendre for Blackwood.

'Understandable, I suppose, for a green girl. But surely you see him differently now? Forgive my bluntness, but I am concerned for your reputation.'

Blanche met his eyes, letting just a little of her confusion show. How did she see Blackwood now? Had it not been for his uncaring attitude in those few minutes before they returned to the ballroom, she would have said that he was everything that she had imagined, and more. But now?

'I.... am considering my opinion. Our conversation this evening was... most interesting. And not quite what I expected.'

Captain Westbury looked ready to press her for more information, and she looked around, desperate to find a way out of this conversation, before she admitted everything to this man. No matter how attractive she found him, his blunt and forceful probing of her private life was not something that she could cope with any longer.

"Now, if you will excuse me, I see that I must rescue my sister, or she will be trapped talking to the chaperones all evening!'

Blanche turned, and sped across the room to where Charlotte was still hopelessly caught in a conversation with Lady Eddleston – who was 90, loved to gossip, and insisted on telling, and retelling, stories from 40 years ago, as if they had happened yesterday. She could only admire Charlotte's endurance, and dedication to upholding the family honour, by being nice to everyone, all the time!

Captain Westbury watched her go, a slight smile touching his face. There was something going on there, and he meant to find out more. Blackwood was a cad, if even half the things said of him were true, and Westbury could not bear the thought of Lady Blanchette with Blackwood. His imagination was quite capable of conjuring up a very wide range of improper things that Blackwood would, almost certainly, like to do with Blanchette, and a rush of fury ran through him at the idea of it.

He forced his fingers to uncurl, before he snapped the stem of the glass in his hand, and silently vowed to watch both of them very closely as this week progressed. He would discover Blanchette's secrets, and protect her from Blackwood if necessary.

Chapter Seven

Blanche's evening had been a whirlwind of emotions. She and Charlotte had both excused themselves and sought their beds early. Charlotte was feeling somewhat depressed and out of sorts after yet another pointless event spent trying, and failing, to have an intelligent conversation with a range of young gentlemen, and Blanche was feeling very conflicted by the events of the ball.

She had experienced many pleasures, and yet she knew, and had been reminded, by Captain Westbury's questions, that she had not made the right choice this time. Even if she had not admitted her behaviour to him, she felt that he had suspected it, and most certainly judged her for it. She had not made the right choice previously, with Charles, either, she now realised, but at least they had been betrothed at the time.

Yet the pleasure had been so intense – surely something so good should not be a terrible sin? At the same time, she realised, somehow it felt as if something was missing, some depth to the whole experience that should have been there, and had not been.

This time, it was perhaps, as if something had been stolen from her, she felt almost used, and as if her liaison was illegitimate and should never have been allowed to happen. It did not matter the selfish pleasure that she had taken from it at the time, it had still been a foolish choice. A huge part of her wished that it had not happened, but there was no changing what had already taken place. She had had intimate relations out of wedlock with James Blackwood, and nothing she could ever say or do would change that immutable fact.

Her attraction to Mr. Blackwood was more deeply rooted than this evening. It had been growing, swelling inside her since she was little more than a girl, putting down roots and nourishing itself on fantasies that she had created from what she read in novels and spoke of in whispered conversation with her sister. When she was too young to be the object of a seduction she had considered him the most handsome and charming man in all the world, delighting her and her parents with his stories of exotic places and his unusual opinions, for which he refused to apologise or feel ashamed.

He was strong and dashing and lived as he pleased, he did not seem to care what others thought of him and he knew what aroused young women, and one could not help but admire all of that in part. Yet at the same time, she had long known, deep down that he was not completely a good man.

He was not nice, or honest, or honourable, and he cared more about his own pleasures and maintaining the dark reputation, that made it so easy for him to exercise fascination in others, (especially nubile young girls) than he did for the wellbeing of his many conquests. That much was painfully obvious now. Yet part of her still wanted him.

What was she to do? Could she be strong, for the rest of this week, if he tried to take advantage of her again? Or would she let her own wanton, lustful nature override her sense again?

She had come to realise tonight, after much consideration, that he had intentionally encouraged her fantasies, her fascination with him, for all those years, simply so that he could, when he chose, take advantage of her. As he had now done.

She was sensible enough, after her failed 'not quite marriage' and after observing the marriages of some of her friends, to know that she would be deluding herself if she tried to believe that she could change him.

Marriage would not reform his character any more than the love of a good woman. He had been this way too long to respond to the advice of others or to compromise for the sake of some girl's opinion. Knowing this did not stop her from still finding Blackwood compellingly attractive.

It would also have been delusion not to acknowledge her attraction to Captain Westbury, although this was now a very complicated phenomenon, working its way through the various alleyways of her mind.

He was probably one of the most handsome men that she had ever met, even more so than her former husband-to-be, who had run off with a governess and left her in disgrace, deeply embarrassed in front of society, and depressed enough to be easy prey to a man like Blackwood.

She had been fascinated by his unassuming nature and his quietly told tales of military heroism. A girlish instinct in her wanted little more than to submit herself to this strong and proud man. But despite that, their conversations had not been all that easy.

He had seemed wary of her and jealous of Blackwood, and had pressed her, as if expecting that she would confess her indiscretions – yet still she felt that she could trust him.

Perhaps he had spent too much time in the company of fellow soldiers and lacked in grace and panache. He seemed to have a sense of humour, and some understanding of ladies, but he was an enigma. She had too many questions over his character and his conduct to unequivocally admit an attraction to herself, though she knew it was there on one level. But that level was very much physical – and she vowed never to let her lustful wanton nature overtake her good sense again!

Her mind was all awhirl, and it seemed that sleep would be a long time coming.

The following morning, Blanche stayed abed late, having only fallen into a fitful sleep as dawn was fast approaching. Upon waking, she felt little enthusiasm for the day – how was she to face either Mr Blackwood or Captain Westbury with a calm face, and adequate social grace?

Once the sun was high outside her windows, and she had heard, drifting up from below, the sounds of the gentlemen setting off to hunt, she dragged herself from her bed, drew back the curtains on what appeared to be a quite disgustingly cheerful sunny day, and rang for Jane to assist her with dressing. She would, she decided, simply not think about how she would greet the two gentlemen, for now. Perhaps breakfast would improve her opinion of the day.

Charlotte looked up from her barely touched plate as her sister entered the breakfast room.

'Why Blanche, you look positively exhausted still – did you not sleep well?'

Blanche selected a small portion of eggs from the wide range of dishes laid out on the sideboard, and sighed as she sat down across from Charlotte. They were alone in the room, and Blanche was relieved that she need not be concerned with social niceties for now.

'I could not sleep. My mind is quite awhirl with the possibilities of the rest of the week. I want so much to take this opportunity to get over the horror of being jilted, and to enjoy myself again, but I am so confused. Both Mr Blackwood and Captain Westbury have shown me some attention, and I simply cannot decide who to like, what I think, what to do!'

Charlotte laughed, and clapped her hands together in some glee.

'See Blanche, I was right to tell you that being a part of this party was a good idea! You complain of a situation that most young ladies we know would love to experience – how jealous they will all be! Why don't you just spend time talking with each of them, enjoy their company, and see what transpires? I cannot imagine that either of them would be so taxing as company that you could not enjoy doing so.'

Blanche sighed, but admitted that, perhaps, Charlotte had the right of it. They finished their breakfast in amicable silence, then sought out the other ladies in the drawing room. A morning of cheerful gossip and embroidery went a long way to restoring Blanche's equilibrium, although she was careful to make no comment when the ladies remarked on how handsome Captain Westbury was.

The gossip then turned to James Blackwood, with one of their neighbours raising his scandalous reputation, whispering of tales heard about his many mistresses. Blanche would, at that point, have liked the floor to open up and swallow her, but was saved from having to make comment by her mother, who quashed the discussion immediately.

"Rubbish" declared lady Derbyshire, "James is a delightful young man, so well-travelled and entertaining, I am sure that is all just foolish fabrication from person's who are jealous of his wealth and experience. I will hear none of it! Let us talk of other things entirely."

Blanche found that, today, she felt little kinship with these twittering sparrows of women. Had she once really enjoyed this silly spying into other's lives? Had she really been so shallow and uncaring, only looking for the thrill of hearing titillating information. Shockingly, she rather thought that she had been exactly like them. Was that, oh terrible thought, was that why Charles had cast her off?

Her gloom of earlier returned, and, pleading a sudden megrim, she hurried from the room. Perhaps if she spent the afternoon in her room, reading, she would feel more like herself. She need not come down for dinner – she could get Jane to bring her a tray.

With that plan in mind, she entered the library, heading straight to the shelves where her favourite books were kept. The sound of the door closing behind her brought her to a sudden stop.

She spun around, to find James Blackwood in front of her, looking at her in a way that was certainly not how a gentleman should look at a lady. Her heart beat faster, and a dark excitement thrummed through her, accompanied by not a little fear.

Unconsciously, she took a step back, to find herself hard up against the bookshelves.

'Good morning Mr Blackwood.' Despite her best efforts, her voice shook a little as she spoke. 'I had thought you out hunting with the other gentlemen?'

"So formal Blanche?" The question was accompanied by a sardonic half smile, and a raise of that very expressive eyebrow of his. He stepped closer, his body almost touching hers, trapping her against the hard shelves behind her. "As it happens, my horse had the inconsideration to throw a shoe, forcing me to return early. But perhaps that is not such a misfortune after all.'

He reached up, and slid his fingers sensually down her cheek, to brush them slowly across her lips. No matter what she thought of his attitude, his proximity was intoxicating, and her body remembered his touch all too well, hear breathing was uneven, and part of her craved more, so much more.

He grinned, certain of himself, all cocksure arrogance.

'It would be a pity to waste this unexpected opportunity', as he spoke, his hands slid caressingly from her shoulders, down over her waist and hips, to cup her buttocks and pull her against him. It was immediately obvious that he was aroused, his manhood hard and ready, pressed against her through the layers of their clothes.

Blanche shivered, aroused despite herself, and horrified that she was. Her hands came up to push against him, and he chuckled, interpreting her reactions as an enthusiasm for his attentions. She was shaking, but no longer from arousal.

'So excited to see me, my 'pure' little lady, with the heart of a whore? Delightful, you have no idea how much that pleases me. So much so, that I believe an immediate repeat of our pleasurable encounter is called for. The gentlemen will not be back for some hours, the ladies are occupied, and the door is locked – I believe that makes the circumstances ideal.'

Blanche pushed against him again, harder, squirming in an attempt to free herself from his hold, but, it seemed, only inflaming his passions further.

'Mr Blackwood! I decline your suggestion. I do not, at this point, wish to repeat our encounter.' She tried for firm, but heard her voice shake as she spoke. He simply laughed, and bent to take her lips in a bruising kiss, lacking all finesse or gentleness, plundering her mouth with his tongue, as his hands hauled her even harder against him.

Taking one hand from her buttock, he started to pull up her skirts, obviously intent on slaking his lust with no concern for her words. Blanche took advantage of that moment, when he had less grip on her, to twist violently sideways and out of his hold. Not fast enough.

He grabbed her arm and twisted her round to hold her against him again, her back pressed against his strong body, and his arm pinning her there, wrapped fully around her waist and trapping her arms against her sides.

Blanche was panting with fear, and an odd and horrifying excitement. When she had thought him mysterious and dangerous, she had not imagined quite this.

Blackwood's other hand came up to her bodice, stroking her breasts through the fabric, then sliding his fingers under the edge of her bodice to pinch at her nipple. She bucked against him, trying to get away, but he laughed again, a cruel laugh, full of his own dark pleasure in what he was doing.

"My dear Blanche, I do so enjoy it when a woman struggles against me. You are such a spirited delight. But you do realise that I will have what I want, don't you? You made your choice when you let Charles take your virginity in the first place. Because now that I know that, and have proven it for myself so delightfully, I can, of course, choose at any time to let the world of society know of your disgrace – subtly of course, but well enough to ruin your reputation forever. And then no-one would ever marry you, would they? And, as I have no desire to marry, once I am bored with you, I may even allow you to marry, and not say a word. But first, I will have what I want - so you will do whatever I say, when it comes to facilitating my pleasure. It is so lovely to know that you can be used, and that, regardless of what you say, I can make you feel pleasure – if I want to be so generous.'

He laughed again, and Blanche realised, with a sinking heart, that there was no escape, that she would do what he wanted. Not because she cared for her own reputation so much, but because such a disgrace would destroy her parents, and taint Charlotte's hopes for marriage as well.

'Enough delightful conversation. It is time for you to provide me a completely different kind of delight, my little whore.'

With another hard pinch to her nipple Blackwood shoved her forward, forcing her to bend over the high padded back of the armchair beside them. She did not fight him, a sense of despair settling in her as he pulled her skirts and petticoats up over her back and slid his fingers through the slit in her drawers.

'Let me make sure that you are ready.' He knelt behind her, one hand on her back to keep her still, and she felt his tongue on her most intimate flesh, brushing her with moistness, and triggering reactions in her body that she could not prevent, using all of his well-practiced skill to prepare her for his cock.

Her mind rebelled but her body did not – she felt numb and her body accepted his thrusts as he sated his lust, pounding into her, with little care for her enjoyment. It was, she realised, all about power – this man enjoyed the power that he had over her – his arousal had nothing to do with affection for her, only with controlling her.

As he pulled from her at the end, capturing his emissions into a handkerchief he held ready, she was grateful at least that he bothered to prevent illegitimate children. Shakily, she pushed herself upright, and set her clothes to rights.

'You may expect me to require your 'co-operation' some further times during this delightful house party, my dear Blanche. I fully intend to enjoy myself while I have the opportunity so easily to hand. Don't look so shocked, my little whore – after all, if you remember, you seduced me…..'

Restored to his usual urbane elegance, he turned from her, so sure of his control as to not feel the need to say or do more, and left the room. Blanche collected the book that she had come for and, megrim now quite thoroughly real, retired to her room.

For the rest of that day, and all of the following, Blanche kept to her room, sending Jane for trays of food and drink when she felt able to contemplate eating, refusing to see anyone, and locking the door against any intrusion. She felt a deep sense of revulsion for herself, for all of the choices that she had made, that had brought her to this point.

Yet she had no choices left. She would not hurt Charlotte any more than she already had. If accepting Blackwood's now loathsome attentions was the price of her family's reputation, she would do so. What horrified her most was that, at least in part, Blackwood's rough handling had excited her, that he was able to make her body react, at least to some extent, regardless of what she wanted.

Surely that was beyond wanton and lustful, and right on the edge, if not over the edge, of perverted.

She cried, she wrote in her journal, she slept and she watched out the window, being careful to stay hidden by the curtains, as the gentlemen rode out to hunt, the ladies took picnics on the lawns, and life went on around her, as if nothing had changed.

James Blackwood laughed and joked with the other men, rode off to hunt, and generally spent the time looking relaxed and rather pleased with himself. She decided that she hated him even more for that.

Captain Westbury looked magnificent. Quiet and authoritative, competent in everything that he did, it was obvious as she watched that the other men respected him, and his honourable behaviour was unquestioned. She knew that she could never have a man like him. Not now, not after what she had done. She was as ruined as a girl could get, and no decent man would ever marry her. That did not stop her heart beating harder each time she saw him through the window, or stop her from imagining what things might have been like, if she had met Captain Westbury before Charles, before any of these sordid things had happened.

She remembered dancing with him at the ball, and wished that she had never let James Blackwood lure her from his arms.

The one question, that her mind skittered away from every time, was how she was going to deal with tomorrow. She could not stay in this room for the rest of the week – her excuse of illness had already worn thin. But once she left this room, she could not know where or when Blackwood might trap her, and demand that she service his lusts. She could lock her room at night, but even that might not stop him – perhaps he could pick locks?

Late on the second day after she had taken to her room, Blanche emerged, having no trouble looking convincingly pale and shaky after her 'illness'. She was, quite simply, terrified, but could hide no longer. If she were to live with the consequences of her actions, it was time to start doing so.

She ventured downstairs to find all of the guests gathered in the drawing room, sipping pre dinner sherry and loudly discussing the day's hunting, and the plans for tomorrow. Blanche paused in the doorway, gathering her nerves and taking in the scene. Her sister looked determinedly cheerful as always, and was listening to hunting anecdotes told by old Lord Miltonhew, her parents were surrounded by their friends and engaged in happy conversation.

Captain Westbury drew her eye, resplendent in uniform and more handsome than ever, apparently discussing the war with some Lords whose sons had also served in France and Spain. Mr Blackwood was the dark to Westbury's light – he stood with a smaller group of men to one side, talking of travel and exotic adventures, making sure that he was the centre of attention. How typical. How could she ever have found him appealing? He was handsome, in his dark and dangerous way, but self-centred and vain in everything that he did.

She felt the last of her young girl's fantasies crumbling away to dust, leaving a much uglier truth revealed before her. She had paused too long. Blackwood saw her. He smiled at her across the room – it was not an attractive smile. He gazed at her in a way that made her feel stripped of her clothes, and ashamed all over again, of everything that she had done.

Taking a deep breath, she moved into the room, choosing to go to her sister, and support her in being polite to the boring elderly guests. Boring old gentlemen were a much safer option than any other in the room.

Her movement brought Captain Westbury's eyes to her, and the sensation was so different from that of Blackwood's gaze, that she faltered a little as she walked. It was warm, and clear, and appeared to convey a genuine concern for her person. At her stumble, he excused himself from his conversation, and advanced to greet her, taking her arm to stabilise her as she recovered.

She leant into him, unable to stop herself, treasuring the momentary sense of security that his touch had brought. Then she pulled herself up. That sense of security was utterly false. She had no security now, there was no help available. She had made her choices, and there was no escaping them.

Captain Westbury looked at her, feeling her pull away, and asked, very quietly "is all well with you now, Lady Blanchette? You seem a little unsteady". His voice washed over her, deep timbred and warm, and she was grateful for his concern. But could admit nothing.

'I am much recovered, thank you Captain Westbury. Though still a little tired I fear. I believe that I will retire early this evening.'

He acknowledged her words with a little bow, stepping back and releasing her arm.

"If I may be of any assistance, you have only to call."

She felt somehow colder for the loss of his touch. Resuming her path to Charlotte, she did not look back or, indeed, anywhere in the room, except at Charlotte.

Westbury watched her go, a slight frown marring his expression, before he returned to his companions. As he turned, he caught Blackwood watching her, with an expression on his face that seemed out of place. It carried echoes of lust, of anger and of something that might be jealousy. He did not like that look. He did not like Blackwood, for that matter, but civility must be maintained.

He was, however, more certain than before that Lady Blanchette was hiding something, something that had to do with Blackwood. He was determined to uncover it, and he had the most disturbing feeling that the time was short to do so.

Dinner passed in a blur for Blanche, she ate little, and was continually aware of the eyes of both Blackwood and Westbury on her. She wanted to run from the room and the effort of staying there and behaving normally was exhausting. When the gentlemen retired to the study for port, she joined the ladies in the drawing room for tea, but struggled to make any conversation at all. After an hour, she felt completely unable to continue, and excused herself.

'I fear that I am very poor company this evening Mother, I believe that I will retire, and hope to be in better spirits tomorrow.'

"Oh my poor child, of course you must go and rest, you must do everything necessary to get yourself well again".

She left the room perhaps faster than was elegant, or appropriate, but she was beyond caring. Taking a deep, relieved breath, she headed upstairs to her room.

The door to the study had been left open a little, as had the windows, to allow some air to flow through, and dispel the aromatic smoke from the cheroots that a few of the gentlemen enjoyed.

James Blackwood had positioned himself in the only chair with a clear view out the door, and down the hallway towards the drawing room door.

After having no access to Lady Blanchette for the last two days, his lust had risen. He did not like being denied. He was, for a fact, not at all used to being denied. It was more common for women to seek his bed than avoid it. Denial was not a sensation that he intended to become familiar with.

When she had arrived in the drawing room before dinner he had been pleased. He was sure to be able to engineer an opportunity to get her alone, and his cock had hardened at the thought. Then Westbury had had the presumption to go to her, and touch her.

His reaction had been strong – he wanted complete control of what was his, did not want any other man touching her. He had caught himself, pasted his mask of civility back into place, and not laid Westbury out on the spot. Although he had wanted to.

It only reinforced his need to have her, to have his pleasure, and to show her once again that she was his, until he decided otherwise.

He had hoped that an opportunity might present itself, and his patience was rewarded when he saw her, an hour or so later, slip out of the drawing room by herself, and head towards the stairs. He excused himself from the conversation and slipped out the door to follow her.

Blanche reached the top of the stairs and turned down the corridor towards her room, she was not concerned when she heard light footsteps, assuming that it was one of the servants on an errand of some sort. She therefore emitted a rather loud squeak of alarm, when a hand grabbed her arm, a squeak that was rapidly cut off by a hand over her mouth.

She was pulled against a hard body, and knew at once that it was Blackwood – there was a distinct smell to him, of cheroots, and brandy, and something a little musty and not quite pleasant underneath it all. 'Shhh' he whispered, as he uncovered her mouth 'you wouldn't want anyone to see us, now would you?'

She shook her head, feeling her body shaking in his grasp, and knowing that her reaction pleased him, and fed his sense of power. He pulled her along the hallway, and through the door of a small storage room, closing the door behind them. Turning, he leant back against the door, effectively locking it with his weight, and looked at her, smiling in that unpleasant way of his.

"We don't have much time, my little whore, the gentle men will be expecting me back at any minute, so I think that I will forgo the niceties this time, and simply take my pleasure of you in the most expedient way possible.'

She watched him, unsure what was coming next, what he meant by those words. He carefully unbuttoned his falls, letting his long hard cock spring free. She shivered again, at the thought of what he might do with her now.

'Kneel' he commanded harshly.

Still puzzled, she did as demanded, finding her face almost hard up against his jutting appendage, in the small space of the storage room. He reached down with one hand, sliding it in the edge of her bodice to find her nipple, and took her hair in his other hand, pulling her head towards him.

'Take it in your mouth, little whore, suck and lick me, now!'

The command shocked her – this was not something that she had done before, or ever imagined doing, and, whilst she could imagine, based on the pleasure that his mouth had given her, that a man would want this, the idea of doing it to him repelled her. She cast about desperately for an idea, for a way out, but none existed, she was trapped.

'Now' he pulled her head harder against him, thrusting himself against her lips. She gasped at the sensation, and he took full advantage of that to push his cock further into her mouth. 'Suck' he commanded, sliding in and out of her mouth, as he had in and out of her body before. Despairing, she obeyed, wanting this done, as fast as possible, wanting to escape him, and his uncaring lust.

He groaned in pleasure as she complied with his orders, and within a few thrusts had spilled his seed in her mouth. She gagged, and turning, spit it forth onto the stacked linens at her side.

She wiped her mouth, and turned to see him, already restored to his sartorial best, watching her with amusement.

'That will do for now, my little whore, but rest assured, I will find a time to be much more leisurely about things, soon.'

He cautiously opened the door a crack, and finding the corridor empty, slipped out and away. She stood, hating him, hating herself, hating the taste of him in her mouth. Her sense of shame and hopelessness redoubled, she crept out, and down the corridor to her room, where she kept her composure just long enough to ring for Jane to help her prepare for bed, and to bring her a cup of chocolate.

Once Jane was gone, and her door locked, she sat shivering in her bed, sipping the chocolate and letting it wash his taste from her mouth. She was horrified anew – he had given up all pretence of wanting to give her pleasure, and was simply using her for his own. He was the most shallow and selfish man she had ever met, and she quietly wept for her blindness in not seeing that before.

Having cried herself to exhaustion, Blanche had slept surprisingly well, dreaming of Captain Westbury and light filled happy days. The happiness lasted but a few minutes after waking, shattered when her memory supplied all of the unpleasant details of the previous evening.

It was obvious that she could not hide, that he would find her regardless and use her as he wished. She was not prone to letting things beat her, although Charles jilting her at the altar had come close.

She would certainly not let this beat her now. If she could just manage to get through the next few days, the house party would end, he would have to leave, and it would be much harder for him to get to her after that. She would do this, would survive this, for Charlotte's sake, of for nothing else.

She rose, rang for Jane, and dressed for the day. The breakfast room was empty, and she was grateful for the chance to simply sit in peace, not needing to converse with anyone, or make an effort to seem happy and interested in the day's activities.

She managed to eat. Although her appetite was small, she knew that keeping up her strength was essential. A flicker of movement caught her eye, and she flinched as someone came through the door, dreading the possibility that it was Blackwood. Relief followed fast, as Captain Westbury greeted her cheerfully.

'Good morrow Lady Blanchette, I trust that you slept well, and are feeling more yourself today?'

Blanche tried to sound sincere as she replied.

"Of a certainty, Captain, a peaceful sleep is always restorative. But is something amiss - are you not hunting this morning?" As she spoke fear flickered in her eyes – if the gentlemen had not gone hunting….. then Blackwood might accost her at any moment.

'Nothing is amiss, do not concern yourself – I had some business to attend to, and chose to deal with that early today. Whilst I do enjoy a good hunt, I am not so obsessed as to not be able to forgo the pleasure when needs must. Now that is dealt with, I can enjoy this repast and take the rest of the day at my leisure.'

She subsided, pushing the last of her food around her plate rather listlessly, but Westbury was not fooled, he had seen the flicker of fear in her eyes, seen her flinch and then recover when he entered the room.

Surely she was not afraid of him? No, he could not countenance that possibility, it must be that she had feared to see someone else enter the room. More secrets. He did not like secrets – he was used to blunt honesty in the field, and found the veiled truths and cunning lies of society remarkably unpleasant.

So, what, or who, was it, that she feared?

Blanche watched him, careful sidelong glances taking the measure of his mood. He was so well made a man, and even frowning as he did now, his face was not threatening. She could not imagine him harming her.

She pushed away the thoughts that compared him to Blackwood, that reminded her of the terrible mistake that she had made, the mistake for which there was no remedy.

Such an honourable man would never consider her worthy of his attention if he knew of her ruin, of her wanton nature and foolish behaviour.

She could never have a man like him – such a man would turn from her in disgust. But still, his presence in the room made her feel safer, and her heart beat faster with a hopeless yearning for his touch.

'Lady Blanchette?'

She had been woolgathering – he had spoken before, and now repeated his enquiry, looking at her in concern.

"Captain," she blushed as she spoke, embarrassed at her lapse "forgive me, my attention had wandered."

'Lady Blanchette, would you do me the honour of showing me the magnificent gardens of your home? It seems that we have this fine morning to ourselves, and it would be a shame to waste the spring sunshine.'

Captain Westbury was more and more intrigued by this woman every time he saw her. More and more concerned as well. Ever since the moment when Blackwood had so rudely drawn her away from him at the ball, she had seemed distant, worried, afraid of shadows almost. He wanted to know why. He felt an unexpected urge to gather her to him, and soothe the look of tiredness and fear from her eyes.

"Why, I would be glad to, Captain."

She rose from the table and placed her hand on his extended arm, smiling as she did so. It was the first unclouded expression he had seen on her face since the moment of their first meeting.

The secluded shade of the winding gravelled walkways through the beautifully laid out gardens produced an immediate sense of relief. Walking through the house, and across the terrace, Blanche had feared to see Blackwood emerge from the direction of the stables and turn his terrible gaze on her. She knew it was foolish to feel so, as he was far from here, hunting with the others, and would not give over that pleasure lightly. But still, the tension did not leave her until they passed out of easy sight of other's eyes.

At first they simply walked, not speaking, appreciating the warmth of the dappled sunlight in the artfully placed small clearings among the leafy trees, and the delicious scents of the beds of carefully tended flowers.

Captain Westbury watched her, watched the glint of the sunlight on her hair, where tendrils of it escaped from her pins, slid out from under her bonnet and drifted to curl over her shoulder. He wanted to touch it, to see if it felt as soft as it looked.

He felt more heated by the warmth of her gloved hand, where it rested on his arm, than by the spring sunshine. He felt.... well he did not quite know what he felt, except that it felt surprisingly like one of those warm and impossible dreams that soldiers have, only to wake to the depressing reality of war. But this was not, he assured himself, a dream.

They came to a clearing with a rustic bench, cleverly placed to provide a view out across the gardens to the lake, yet not be overlooked easily. Without words, in perfect accord, they stopped, and sat, close against each other. Blanche did not want to speak, did not want him to speak, did not want to break the magic of the moment, this moment in which she felt safe, and as if anything was possible. She pushed her bonnet back, and let the sun touch her skin.

His arm slid around her, and her head tilted to rest on his shoulder, as if it was the most natural thing in the world that they should be at such intimate ease with each other. She allowed herself, for just this moment in time, to absorb every little thing about him, the smell of his cologne, the slight roughness of his coat against her cheek, the hard strength of his muscular chest beneath it, the strong beat of his heart, beating as hard as hers and the safe, protecting feel of his arm around her.

The moment seemed to stretch out, and she did not move as he raised his hand and gently caressed her face, tilting her chin up as he bent to softly kiss her lips. There was nothing of demand in that kiss, more a savouring of sweetness, a delicate exploration of her mouth, and all the sensations bound up in soft lips and warm tongue.

She melted into it, savouring him in return, and thought with wonder how different this kiss was from any that she had ever experienced before.

But with that thought, reality came crashing back, as the truth of those kisses that she had felt before reminded her how impossible this was, how hopeless. For she could not have this, she, ruined woman that she was, could not have a man like this, could not risk him finding out the truth.

Nor could she bear to lead him on, to allow him to believe that they might have something together, only to watch his gentleness and care turn to revulsion once he knew. As surely he would know, the first time that he took her to his bed.

With a little cry, she pushed herself away from him, despair in her eyes. 'We cannot…. I should not have…….' Shaking her head she stood, and stepped back. He reached out a hand to her, but, at the look on her face, let it drop, his eyes full of confusion, and some hurt.

'Lady Blanchette, I am so sorry, I never meant…. ' At his words, she gave one small sob, turned and fled back towards the house, the sound of her name on his lips following her into the trees.

He stood, watching her go, internally berating himself. He had meant simply to enjoy her company, to talk with her a little, outside the rather stifling confines of the house, and well away from that bounder, Blackwood. But it had been too much, had seemed so right, that, when she leant into him like that, so trusting, he could not help himself. And so he had betrayed that very trust, obviously pushing her too far, too fast.

He was coming to understand that he cared about this girl a great deal, rather more than he had cared about any of the women in his past. And now he had made her run from him. He was an unmitigated fool!

A soldier did not run from his mistakes. He squared his shoulders, took a deep breath, and wound his way back through the trees, considering his strategy. He still wanted to know her secrets, to know why she had seemed so afraid this morning, to regain her trust, and repair the damage that he had just done. And, whispered the little voice in his mind, to kiss her again, and have her stay.

The afternoon had passed in a blur for Blanche, and she was glad of the need for planning and organising, which gave her something to do, and kept her mother too distracted to look at Blanche too closely. Her mother had decided that tomorrow they should have another ball, before most of the guests departed on the following day. Apparently she had received news that some important guests, who had been unable to attend until now, would arrive just for a day or two, tomorrow.

For Lady Derbyshire, that was an excellent excuse for another celebration. The Cook and the Housekeeper were close to hysterics at the news, and the staff were in uproar with the rushed preparations.

Captain Westbury, upon reaching the house, had been almost knocked from his feet by two footmen, who were struggling to relocate a rather alarmingly large marble flower urn to the ballroom, at Lady Derbyshire's order.

They were most apologetic, extremely grateful that it was the polite and unflappable Captain that they had collided with, rather than one of the more acerbic guests, and cheerfully informed Westbury of the new plans afoot.

Faced with an afternoon of feminine bustle and chaos belowstairs, he rapidly amended his plans, and took himself to the stables. A good long ride would flush the cobwebs from his thinking, and give him time to think through the situation, and find some sort of strategy that might work. He would, he had decided, do everything that he could to convince Lady Blanchette to accept his suit.

Some hours later, much refreshed, and polished to perfection in his best evening dress, Captain Westbury felt up to the challenge that he was sure the next few hours would present. He would, no matter what, manage to speak with Lady Blanchette, to get her, somehow, to confide her secrets. He would also be watching Blackwood closely – he did not, in any way, trust the man.

Stepping into the drawing room, where the company was gathered for a pre-dinner drink, his eye went immediately to Lady Blanchette. She looked remarkable, more beautiful than ever, her lustrous hair swept up and artfully tangled through with ribbon, her gown a deep sapphire blue that made her beautiful eyes seem even more intense. She quite took his breath away.

He realised, with a start, that he had been staring, rather rudely, and turned his gaze away, only to find Blackwood glaring at him, with a look that could quite possibly melt a bullet in flight. A look that did not bode well for the evening's polite conversation.

"Ah Captain," Lord Derbyshire waved him over "you missed a capital hunt this morning ! We started in the north coppice and......"

Westbury tried his best to appear to listen, as Lady Blanchette's father regaled him with the entire sequence of events of the day. His attention, however, was elsewhere. Lady Blanchette had been speaking to one of the elderly Ladies, and turning, moved towards Lady Charlotte. Blackwood smoothly removed himself from the rather raucous conversation of the younger set, and, equally smoothly, diverted Lady Blanchette from her path, taking her elbow to draw her over to the terrace doors.

She hid it well, but Westbury still saw the reaction in her body when Blackwood touched her, and the rather desperate glance that she threw over her shoulder, as he drew her aside. No-one else noticed anything amiss. It just seemed that two well acquainted young people were conversing politely, in full view of the room.

It was certainly not, to Westbury's keen eye, polite. Blackwood kept a firm grip on her arm, carefully standing so that his body almost completely blocked the view of it. Lady Blanchette's shoulders sagged, and she appeared most unhappy with whatever he was saying.

But, for some reason he could not fathom, she did not pull away from the bounder, did not demand that he unhand her, did nothing but listen. Doubt crept in to Westbury's mind. Could he be wrong? Could it be that she liked, even wanted, the attentions of the cad? Why else would she accept such improper handling? More than ever, he needed to talk to her, to know the truth, no matter how much the truth might hurt.

Moments later Blackwood released her and, with barely a nod, sauntered off back to the conversation he had left earlier. He looked smugly pleased with himself – an expression that Captain Westbury found he would like to wipe from Blackwood's face... with a fist.

Blanche looked somewhat shaken as she reached Charlotte, who gave her a considering look, but said nothing, beyond commenting on how well the colour of her dress suited her. They conversed for a while discussing all of the arrangements for tomorrow night's surprise ball, and speculating as to who the new important guests might be, as their mother had coyly refused to tell them.

Blanche carefully manoeuvred them, with the excuse of obtaining a drink, to quite the opposite side of the room from Blackwood, so that all of the guests, and a few potted palms too, were between them and the group where he stood. She felt better when he could not easily watch her. Her arm still felt soiled somehow, where he had held her, and her mind more so, by what he had said. All the while smiling, as if discussing the weather, he had informed her that he would come to her chamber tonight, and that he expected her to be ready and waiting to serve his needs.

He had looked across the room at Charlotte, and, quirking an eyebrow at her, had said 'your poor dear sister would be so terribly shocked if she knew what a little whore you are. And it would ruin her reputation forever, should anyone else find out.' There was nothing subtle about his meaning.

'Oh Blanche, you do still look so tired. You must make sure to rest properly tonight, so that you can enjoy the ball tomorrow!'

Charlotte held Blanche's hands between hers, looking so genuinely concerned for her sister that it tore at Blanche's heart.

She was saved from replying when Charlotte was summoned to her mother's side, going with good grace, but a little huff of frustration. Blanche looked up, desperate to seek safety in conversation, with someone, anyone, anyone but Blackwood. Looked up - straight into the brilliant blue eyes of Captain Westbury, who had magically appeared in front of her. Had she summoned him, like a knight to protect her, just with her thoughts? She pushed the whimsy aside, and smiled at him.

Right now, no matter how her heart hurt, no matter how strongly she had resolved, this afternoon, that she would not speak to him, not encourage him, she could not push him away now.

She wanted, rather, to cling to him, her relief at having someone to speak to profound. There was, she realised, something odd in his expression, as if he were angry with her. Well, that was not unreasonable, given that she had kissed him this afternoon, then pushed him away and run from him. Oh, she felt such a fool.

His normally sunny eyes were wintry, and he spoke in a somewhat harsh tone.

'After our conversation at the ball, I would not have expected you to allow yourself to be drawn aside by Mr Blackwood again. Could it be that, despite what you said, you enjoy his attentions?'

Blanche gasped, shocked that he could interpret what he had seen in that way, and he paused, seeing the seemingly genuine shock in her eyes. His anger pushed him on though - he had to know the truth.

'Perhaps that little confidence that you shared with me is not the whole of it? Perhaps he has taken advantage of your infatuation rather more than I had thought, or….. is this your choice, has he engaged your affections truly? Is that really what you want in a man? Most of the gentlemen present would consider you to be a most desirable match, perhaps even offer a proposition of marriage should you encourage them in the slightest, even given your previous disgrace. Nevertheless, if it were to be discovered that you had cavorted, shall we say, with a bounder like Blackwood, outside the realms of holy matrimony, why then that would present something of a problem, would it not? Of course, I am simply expressing comment on what might happen, should such a thing be suspected – I am sure that such a well-bred young lady as yourself would never allow herself to be placed in such a position.'

'I suppose it would Captain, should such a thing happen' she replied, her breath a little ragged.

Oh this was awful! The one man she most desperately wished to have care for her, was obviously already judging her, even without knowing the full truth of her depravity. Oh what a terrible mistake she had made, jeopardizing her future prospects, her potential relationships with decent, handsome men, like this Captain, for the sake of a few moments of lust.

And now she was trapped by her own foolishness, ruined beyond repair.

'- and if such a discovery were to be made after a marriage had been arranged, why then that would be the doom of any hopes of securing a proposal in the future and of your position in society as well as that of your family.'

'Yes sir, yes it would!' the tension was unbearable. It was clinging tight to her like a bodice that didn't fit. She was burdened and had to lighten the load. The last few days of dark secret despair, with no one to speak of it to, weighed on her. If the Captain already thought the worst, already despised her for her behaviour, then nothing she did could change that. He was an honourable man, even if he knew, she was sure that he would not reveal his knowledge to the world.

She would cope, if he turned away from her in horror, just so long as her family were not ruined by her folly. She must confess, must trust someone, and unburden herself!

For some reason she felt that she could trust this man, regardless of all that had happened between them, and, somehow, not being honest with him seemed a more terrible crime than exposing her folly to his censure.

'Oh Captain!' she said at last. 'Captain, I fear that I have made a grave error. Can you find it in your heart to forgive me? Is there any honour in me worth preserving?' he looked down at her, at first disapprovingly, but then with a wry little smile and a raise of his eyebrow.

'That remains to be seen' he said to her, unsmiling. 'However, not all men are unfeeling brutes who will not forgive an impressionable young lady the slightest indiscretion. Passion is a strange and powerful force, and there are still some willing to fight to excuse it, and to restore some honour to a lady's reputation.'

'You have found me out, sir' she said, although by this point she did not really need to. 'I did allow passion to overcome me with Mr. Blackwood, in a most inappropriate manner. I fear that his experience at raising passion in women was too much for me. I regret it profoundly, but he has taken most unseemly pleasure in making me aware of the fact that if word ever gets out I, and my family, will be ruined in the eyes of society! He…. He…. He has used that fact to compel me to further intimacy with him, whenever he has been able to make the opportunity.'

Her breathing was coming hard, her face had gone white with fear as she spoke, and her hands clenched in the folds of her beautiful gown.

'Egads! Blackwood is more of a cad and a bounder than even I had thought. Well then…' he spoke with a new found sense of purpose. 'There is only one thing for it. For your sake, and for the sake of all happy and decent futures, I will do what I must.'

She looked up, confusion in her eyes, as he turned from her, and strode purposefully over to where Blackwood stood, looking barely interested in the young men's talk of hunting and gambling.. She watched him tap Blackwood on the shoulder, draw him aside, and then say a few words to him discreetly, in his ear. Blackwood started, looking very displeased, then stilled.

The pair left together, but not before each of them threw her a glance, Blackwood one of malice and hate, Westbury a steely look that seemed determined to convey some sense of hope. She slumped into a chair, hiding behind the potted palms, feeling very confused and very conflicted.

Chapter Eleven

As she pored over her journal, trying to get all of these thoughts out without spilling ink all over herself, there was a knocking at the door, and Smithers, the family butler answered when she asked who was there. She unlocked the door and he entered, looking slightly askance at the fact that the door had been locked, but much too reserved to enquire about it.

He was a tall and grave looking man, with the tact of a veteran servant. He held out a small tray, with a note on top.

'A correspondence for you, my Lady, from young Captain Westbury.'

'Thank you Smithers, that will be all.' She lifted the paper from the tray, cautiously, almost as if it might burn her. With a slight bow the butler left, leaving her feeling mightily confused. What could the note possibly say? Was the Captain also proposing a salacious liaison?

Would that be a terrible mistake, or was that secretly what she desired? NO! That was her wanton nature speaking – she refused to think that way. And surely, after the way that he had left her tonight, he would no longer desire her in any way – she had seen the disgust in his eyes – there was no hope there.

She locked the door again, then, hands shaking with nervous energy, she opened and read the short note, scribbled in the hand of a man more used to writing hasty notes on a battlefield than to writing sentimental or poetic verses:

> *I have pledged myself to your honour, and it is*
> *to be pistols at dawn. We shall be down by the*
> *old pine tree in the grounds.*
>
> *Yours,*
>
> *H W*

A strange blend of excitement and horror ran right through her. A duel! And all on her account! She could not but feel moved by Captain Westbury's gesture, and yet feel awkward that it should be happening at all. That he should so choose to defend her honour, knowing how sullied that honour was, even after she had pushed him away this afternoon in the gardens, amazed her, she did not understand at all. Unable to decide what on earth she could do, beyond rising before dawn to sneak out to see the result of her terrible mistake, and more conscious than ever of the strange and foolish ways of the heart, she lay down and tried as hard as she could to get a little sleep.

The conciseness of the Captain's missive brought a faint smile to her face as she gazed at the ceiling, waiting for sleep to arrive.

It seemed to have the tone of a military directive. *It is to be pistols at dawn. Ready yourselves.* Stoic and unshakable. And yet she couldn't help speculate, as she dozed off, what chimaera of hopes and fears breathed life into these words. Was he not apprehensive *at all*?

Perhaps the message was merely functional, and he gave no consideration to the artful communication of feelings. Perhaps, as she briefly recalled him mentioning earlier in the evening, his emotions had been numbed and tamed by years of warfare.

But speculations tempted her, and she pictured him frowning as he wrote the message, without prevarication; without anxiety, but with just a hint of sentimentality, just for her. But for all its confidence, were there not some whispers of a gentle, hopeful soul that could be inferred?

What hadn't he written, and why? *I have pledged myself to your honour*, she heard over and over as she drifted in and out of sleep. How dependable and safe words seemed to sound when they came from his lips! One could almost touch and embrace his utterances for how solid they were, she thought. Every so often, the initial element of horror she had felt when she first received the correspondence surged back up through her, from where she had tried to swallow it down. She struggled to sleep despite the tumult of emotions, yet it was nigh on impossible, so vertiginous was the excitement of a pledge to her honour; so deep the fear of gunshots at sunrise.

After what could have been minutes or hours, she heard the first lark, and struggled to work out whether she had managed to sleep or not.

But as the pale half-light of pre-dawn edged through her window, and as the events of the previous night crystallized into focus in her mind, she realised what she had to do. It was but a ten minute walk to the pine tree that Captain Westbury had alluded to in his message, which, she noticed with a start, was scrunched up in her exertion-blanched fist where she had clutched it anxiously all night. It would be less than half an hour until dawn. The men would doubtless already be there by the time she arrived, checking their firearms.

She would have little time to adequately prepare herself for the coming rendezvous, and people would utterly disapprove of her presence at the duel, but in that piercing clarity that only fatigue seems to proffer, she knew that she had to watch it happen, had to take at least that much responsibility for the consequences of her actions. Had to be there – because she could imagine only grief resulting – her heart clenched at the thought of either of them hurt or killed. No matter how much she might despise James Blackwood at this moment, he did not deserve death, just because she had been overcome by her own lust.

She rose, resolved to escape the house undetected and to observe the conflict from the hillock that overlooked the expanse upon which that Scots pine towered and brooded.

She hastily dressed in a simple day dress and thrust her hair under a shawl, hoping to be taken for a maid if she were to be spotted, and exited the house through the servants' door. As she rushed through the dewy, crepuscular morning, stifling groans as she stumbled on tufts of grass, near invisible in the pre-dawn light, nightmare images of the possible outcomes of the impending scene danced through her thoughts.

92

How could she be expected to react to the news of a defeated, perhaps slain, rival for her affections? Was this not a rather joyless affair, no matter the result?

Did Captain Westbury expect her to come? Did Blackwood know of this message? Was this merely some strange masculine ruse to test her interest?

She reached the hillock and crept up through the bracken, and, sure enough, she saw in the dim dawn light, across an expanse of lawn, five figures standing rigid under the branches of a pine tree, as if extensions of its brittle limbs.

She could not, however, pick out who was who. Who were the seconds, who the fifth figure? A doctor, she supposed.

She became aware of a rising wind, still chill at this time of year, and began to shiver, so she ventured to move down the slope to escape the wind, and find a better vantage to view the scene, supposing that she was unlikely to be seen among the foliage. She crouched behind a shrouding bush and saw the gilded epaulettes of Captain Westbury glint very briefly, and a few yards from him, Blackwood whispering something in his Second's ear.

She could now see who was there. It seemed that the staff had been pressed into duty as Seconds, and rightly nervous they looked as a result. The tired-looking head gardener, Mr Blyth, a stout Cheshireman, was standing as Second for Blackwood, and Jamison, the Stablemaster, was standing as Second for the Captain. That, at least, gave her confidence that this would be a fair contest – neither of the longstanding and loyal servants would permit anything underhanded.

The village doctor was the fifth man, and he looked extremely disapproving about the whole process, but she knew him to be a good man, who would heal any damage if he possibly could.

Blackwood's lips were moving, but Blanche could not hear what was being said. She suspected he was discussing the rules of engagement, since Captain Westbury stood still and calm, listening respectfully, while Mr Blackwood paced to and fro in agitation. After perhaps five minutes, pale dawn had arrived. Mr Blyth and Jamison nodded at Blackwood and the Captain.

Blanche then jumped as Mr Blyth suddenly yelled, 'Back to back, gentlemen! Ten paces on my count, then turn and fire!' The duellists approached and faced one another, their guns now behind their backs, and abruptly turned around. Captain Westbury was now facing Blanchette from some thirty yards away. In time to Blyth's count, he took ten deliberate paces towards her, his body carried with physical eloquence; his firearm behind his back. But she became suddenly aware that he could now easily see her among the glistening wet leaves. His eyes narrowed for a moment and his lips made the unmistakeable shapes of the word, 'Blanchette...' Their eyes connected after Westbury's sixth step. They gazed at each other as he moved toward her, and Blanche now felt the strong desire to rush through the clear air, risking a wayward bullet, just to embrace this man, whose eyes rested warmly on her chill-pinched face.

At the tenth pace, Mr Blyth roared, "Turn and fire!"

Blackwood had turned and shot before Blyth had finished the first word.

But the bullet sailed past its target and produced a loud crack in the bushes but a yard from Blanche's crouched vantage point, in response to which she could not control issuing a sharp scream which reverberated across the clearing.

It was the first time that she had noticed fear in the Captain's eyes, as he took a pace forward and called.

'My Lady!'

Blanche stood, now blushing, and called out shakily.

"The projectile missed both you and I, sir, and has found its resting place in the trunk of this unfortunate sapling."

She thought that she saw a flicker of a smile pass over Westbury's lips, as he turned and faced his opponent.

"Captain Westbury, you must fire, sir." Jamison announced, eyeing Blanche warily as she walked towards the assembled men.

Blanche looked past the Captain's unwavering frame, to see a fuming Blackwood.

Captain Westbury raised his pistol and pointed it at Blackwood, his arm straight and unmoving. Blackwood squirmed, but held his ground.

Blanche stopped in her tracks and held her breath.

"Ladies should not be present at duels! It is a most scandalous distraction! Did you invite her, sir? May the devil take you, Westbury, for this sabotage! Go on, you dog," Blackwood called out, from his position twenty paces from the Captain, "show us your mettle, you cowardly saboteur!"

"I am inclined to remind you, Mr Blackwood," Mr Blyth said sternly, and without bothering to affect a more genteel accent, "that gentlemanly and civilised manners comprise the soul of this activity..."

"To Hell with you, cur," Blackwood raged, as he stood, shuddering in the wind. Or perhaps shaking with fear.

The Captain, slowly but decidedly, then lowered his firing arm a little and, with telling accuracy, fired his shot straight into the earth a yard from Blackwood's right foot. Blackwood had been spared – it was very, very obvious, however, that it was by the Captain's choice, not from any lack of ability to make the shot.

"What unconscionable cowardice and hypocrisy!" Blackwood shrieked, beginning to look desperate. He then saw the look of distaste on Blanche's face and attempted to recover from his fit of anger.

"I feel it would be only fair," he began with serpentine composure, "that this duel be restarted, since the delightful, but unwitting distraction of Lady Blanchette..."

' happened after your shot had been fired, and can in no way be said to be responsible for your failure to hit me'. Westbury responded at exactly the same moment that Mr Blyth said "I'm afraid, sir, that would be most irregular".

Blyth, to Blanche's amusement and astonishment, appeared to be stifling a yawn as he responded to his superior, the vexed and reddening Blackwood. Clearly keen to regain his bed, Blyth gathered the two pistols in discreet silence, and headed back inside.

'Rest assured Blackwood, should I ever hear of you speaking ill of this Lady, or of you doing anything to her detriment, in any way, I will hunt you down. And next time I will not be merciful, and I will not miss.' Captain Westbury's voice was cold and hard as he spoke.

Blackwood, fuming, acknowledged this statement with a curt nod and turned, throwing her a covetous and furious glare, before disappearing over the hill, ranting and mumbling to himself, his nerves clearly shot through.

'Your courage and dignity are an example to all Englishmen, Captain Westbury. I cannot thank you enough for choosing to champion my honour, especially as you know just how sullied it is.'

'Please' replied the soldier, still impassive and unflappable '- do not flatter me unnecessarily, it is not what I require. I had merely hoped to prevent a young lady from becoming disgraced in the eyes of society. I trust that my efforts were not in vain.'

'Not at all sir! I must trust that Blackwood will heed your words, and not speak of this again. You have saved me from despair and my family from ruin in the eyes of society.'

She rushed towards him, carried forward by an unseen force that swelled within her, beneath that modest dress, and plunged her into his arms. He caught her to him, and very deliberately bent to kiss her. The kiss began gently, but rapidly escalated in intensity, as the fear of the last hours dissolved in the certainty that Westbury was here, alive still, and in her arms.

Blanche knew suddenly that this was the man whom she truly loved.

The James Blackwoods of the world could keep their sordid seductions and uncaring attitudes - to find herself in the arms of a man of integrity and honor, whose word she could trust, was what she had, deep down, always desired.

Captain Westbury's composure was, finally, disrupted. His breathing was fast, and he looked at her with undisguised hunger in his eyes. It seemed at last that his bluff, soldierly façade was cracking, and she was at last getting some glimpse of the man beneath, who felt and dreamed and throbbed, just like anybody else.

He returned her kisses manfully, as he had returned fire in the earlier duel, his tongue more direct than James Blackwood's, but no less stimulating to a young lady on a chilly May morn. She was swept up in his powerful arms and felt that this moment ought to last forever.

Blanche hesitated at first, to do more than simply melt into his kiss, but as the arousal rose in her body, his kiss seeming to spark reactions everywhere, felt confident enough to provoke her handsome Captain further, to allow herself just a little indulgence of her own desires, knowing instinctively that this man would never use her the way that Blackwood had.

She allowed her hand to stray a little below his strapping waistline, towards his breeches and the hard ridge of his manhood, pressing so delightfully against her body as he held her.

She slid her fingers against him, feeling his shape through the taught cloth of his breeches, and knew at once that she had him entranced, as his breath came on a gasp and his lips came down on hers again, plundering the softness of her mouth, as she drove his body to distraction.

The solider stood to attention, tall and firm, inflated with pomp and ceremony, ready for action – she was amused at the image in her mind, even as she was aroused by it.

It took only a little of her intuition to sense forces swelling up inside him, as they were swelling in her, hot need and almost animal lust, fluids and feelings desperate to burst forth between them.

As she had intended, Captain Westbury pulled her harder against him. She was happy now to have brought these instincts out in him, and the lustful wanton in her wanted to submit to this need, to be taken by him, right now. The cold wind had ceased to matter, and all she wanted was his touch.

She had, she thought, managed to bring out this whole new side of his nature, and she rejoiced in knowing that he felt about her so strongly.

She needed this in a man, she now realised, this intensity of physical desire for her, but she needed it accompanied by true care, by love, not as just a sating of the body's needs.

He brought her whole body to him, pressing his maleness against her, hard and forceful. She could feel it through the layers of their clothing, the bulging, turgid shape she had called into service between the Captain's legs.

His kisses, mixed with little nipping bites, brushed down her neck with an energy and passion that she had presumed was the monopoly of more polished lovers, but she realised, perhaps he was in that category – she knew so little of his experience! His bluff exterior may cover hidden depths, which she could not wait to explore.

Regardless, his kisses stirred in her the same bubbling, trembling warmth and wetness that she had experienced with her roguish seducer that first evening in the Library, before his true nature had been revealed. She felt no fear of him, no revulsion for any part of him. Her entire being yearned for his touch, longed to obey his orders.

Westbury, her Henry, the man who had addressed that note to her, fought for her, dazzled her with his looks and grace, was now providing her with greater pleasure than she had ever imagined, just from his kiss.

She wrapped her arms around him, like ivy climbing up a tall, strong tree, surrendering herself to his touch. His hands roamed over her body, caressing her softly and sending tingles up to her breasts and down to her womanhood. His hand hitched up her skirts, as the need to touch her more intimately drove him.

She let out a gasp 'Henry…' and lifted her head back from their kiss to look him directly in the face. He was all so perfect - his sculpted face, golden hair and broad shoulders. His hands already under her skirts, he grabbed her firmly by the buttocks and pulled her close again. She was shaking, not with the cold but from the sheer anticipation of what she knew surely was to come.

He surprised her. With a deep shuddering breath, he dropped his hands from her, and moved back a scant few inches, and stood, breathing hard. Looking deep into her amazing cerulean eyes, he spoke. So dazed was she with passionate need, that it took a few moments for his words to sink in.

'I will not continue any further, no matter how deeply I desire you.' He said, his face touching hers. 'It is not my intention to risk life and limb for a lady's honour and then to violate it myself. I shall do what I had hoped I might eventually do, when I received an invitation to this very party' and then, with a look of regretful determination, he took a further step back.

For a moment, Blanche was bitterly disappointed.

She did not care for any silly notions about 'honour' any more, what she wanted was to feel, and to love, and to experience the highest of pleasures with her dashing officer of the guards!

Had she done something wrong? What on earth had come over him? Or was she being terribly foolish again, and letting her lusts overcome her?

The very next second she had all of her answers in one. Captain Westbury dropped onto one stout knee and his face finally cracked into a pure smile, clean and pearly:

'Lady Blanchette, will you be my bride?' she almost swooned with shock and awe. At last!

'Oh yes! Yes I will!' she declared, tears of joy swelling in her eyes. What a man! Heroic, strong, romantic and capable! He was what she had always wanted, needed, even. As he rose to his feet, he kissed her again, with loving passion, and she allowed him to pull her into his arms.

She looked up at him; he looked just as good from this angle as from every other. Her head rested perfectly against his shoulder, and the strong beat of his heart echoed in her ear.

'Now my dear', he said, full of joyful confidence and with a twinkle in his eye, 'we shall find a little tea and some breakfast. But first, perhaps, we should find somewhere discreet to relieve each other's need, at least a little....' His very words brought her almost to a quivering climax, and she walked up the hillock, back towards the house, with him, happier and more satisfied than she had ever been in all her life.

They snuck in through the servant's door, and she led him to an unused guest room, at the furthest end of the least used wing of the house. Laughing, they slipped through the door, and locked it, to fall onto the bed, already kissing. There was nothing manipulative or posed about Henry's response and actions – it was abundantly clear to her that he wanted her with the same desperation as she wanted him.

Their hands roamed each other's bodies and she revelled in how different this felt from anything that she had experienced before. She could stand it no longer – her fingers slid under the edges of his jacket, and down over his muscled abdomen to where the buttons of his falls stood strained by the pressure that his hardness put on them. Undoing them as fast as she could, she gasped as his kisses moved down her neck, to tease her hardened nipples through the thin fabric of the day dress.

At the same time, his fingers found the laces of the dress, and deftly undid them, allowing it to a slide from her shoulders and reveal her beautiful breasts to his gaze.

She gasped as his tongue delicately traced the edge of her nipple, and reached for him again. He moaned his pleasure against her skin as her fingers finally found his cock, and stroked along the silken skin of its hard length.

His hands grasped her skirts, drawing them up to her waist in one quick movement, as they slid to lie fully on the bed, and she gasped again as the cool morning air touched the wet folds of her most intimate flesh.

'Oh Blanche, you are so beautiful.' His words drifted warm breath across her, bringing her to a quivering height of sensitivity, just before his skilful tongue found the nub of her pleasure and began to work gently to drive her need even higher. She clung to him, pulling him to her, as her hips lifted and drove her against his working tongue. In all too short a time, she found herself cresting the wave of her pleasure, crying out his name as she came apart under his touch.

He held her to him as she came back to herself, watching her with such caring and love in his blue eyes that the contrast to her experiences with Blackwood was enough to make her almost cry with her relief. Gently, she reached for him again, her fingers finding his cock again, and stroking over it wonderingly – he felt so different, and she wanted him so much. The difference, she realised, with sudden clarity, was that she loved this man, as well as lusting after him most intensely.

He went to pull away a little, but Blanche drew him to her, pulling him down over her, kissing him.

'Love me, Henry, please. I want you with all my heart.'

He needed no further encouragement, and shifted to slide himself into her, with one long slow thrust, a moan of deep pleasure forcing itself through his lips as he did, echoed by her own cry of delight.

Their eyes locked as he began to move inside her, and she marvelled again at how wonderfully different this was, at how much she wanted to give this man pleasure in return. Then all thought fled as her pleasure built again and the world shattered, his cries mingling with hers as he pulled from her at the last moment.

They lay in each other's arms, content and happy, until, after some time, Henry raised himself on an elbow, and looked at her smiling.

'That, Blanche, was quite the most intense pleasure that I have ever felt, although I must apologise for the rushed nature of this today. I fear that my desperate need for you led me to not spend as much time as I should have on your pleasure. I will do better next time, I promise you my love.'

She looked at him, wonder in her eyes, that he should want her, love her, even knowing what she had done. And that with him, this intimacy should be so different, so very much more, than it had been before, with either Charles or Blackwood. He shifted, almost uncomfortable at the intensity of her gaze, then smiled.

'Shall we go and find that breakfast now, my love?'

They left the room hand in hand.

Chapter Twelve

'I say Blackwood' said Lord Derbyshire a little later that day, chewing his way through a scone over tea in the breakfast room. '- I must say you look as if you haven't slept a wink! I trust the room and bed are to your satisfaction, I can have you moved if you'd like?'

'They are most satisfactory sir, fear not' replied Blackwood, distractedly. The rogue did certainly look worse for wear that afternoon, with grey-black bulges under his eyes and his hair quite out of place, despite the best efforts of his manservant.

Derbyshire's questions demonstrated that word of the duel under the pine tree had not yet got out. Hopefully, he pondered, it would stay that way.

'I regret that I am only a light sleeper, as the Sultan of Aleppo once found to his cost. My slumber is easily disrupted by birds you see, I can often hear them twittering in the small hours, distracting me...'

'Well we can't be having that!' declared Derbyshire at once. 'I can send Blyth out to scare 'em off if you'd like! He's rather a good shot I believe!'

'That will not be necessary.' Mumbled Blackwood, already bored by this dialogue. He did not bother to point out to his host the futility of trying to improve his guests' sleep with the noise of gunshots. 'I am quite used to sleeping little. Indeed, rest is not, in my humble opinion, the principle purpose of the bedchamber.'

'Ah, I quite see what you mean sir!' Derbyshire replied, with a wink and a knowing pat on the shoulder. 'Precisely what you mean! Reading, of course! There is nothing like the pleasure of a good book before bed, good stirring stuff that stimulates the senses. I have often seen fit to sacrifice sleep myself for the sake of an especially riveting chapter!'

'Yes, my Lord' Blackwood replied, suppressing a sarcastic groan, 'that is precisely what I meant.'

"Well Blackwood, get some food into you, I assume you will be joining us for the hunt this afternoon?   I'm off to see that everything is in readiness.' Lord Derbyshire rose, smiling, and headed for the door.

As he stepped into the hall, he almost collided with Blanche and Captain Westbury. They were considerably better turned out than Blackwood.

Blanche had changed into a sumptuous yellow-cream dress for the morning's conversation, while Westbury had managed to buff up his hair and uniform perfectly. For two people who had also slept very little last night, they looked positively radiant, and were rather pointedly holding each other's hands.

'Pardon me for interrupting Lord Derbyshire.' Westbury said. 'If we might have a word with you, in your study?'

"Of course, of course, what's this all about then?" Lord Derbyshire led them through the study door, and turned to them enquiringly.

'Sir, I have asked Lady Blanchette to marry me, and she has done me the honor of accepting. I hope that you will grant your approval.'

The old earl seemed quite taken aback, and looked at them both consideringly.

'Why...' he blurted. He couldn't refuse them, could he? 'This is rather sudden! Blanchette, are you certain? Is this what you want?'

'Oh yes, father, yes, it is everything that I want' replied Blanche in a clear voice that trembled with happiness at the edges.

"Then of course! Of course you can marry, a most suitable match! Certainly, you have my blessing. And you and I shall have to get better acquainted, Captain Westbury. Tell me my lad, do you hunt often?"

'Why yes sir, it is one of my principle diversions.'

"Capital, capital! But I think that you had best go and tell your mother and sister now, Blanchette. They will never forgive you if you don't tell them straight away!"

They left the room, Lord Derbyshire back to arranging hunting parties, and Blanche and the Captain to seek out her mother and sister. They found them in the drawing room, conversing with a number of guests. Blanchette could barely wait to speak.

'Mama, Captain Westbury and I have an announcement we wish to make. The Captain has asked me to marry him, I have accepted, and Papa has approved the match. We are now engaged to be married.'

There were a few sudden gasps around the room, followed by a courteous but genuine applause. Blanche could not help but notice a few envious glances, from the young ladies present, at the sight of her handsome fiancée in his splendid uniform. He was everything that most young women wanted – handsome, heroic, and the heir to the Bevington fortune as well.

'We shall start making the necessary arrangements at once!' Lady Derbyshire cried. 'It shall be the finest wedding the County of Derbyshire ever saw, and no mistake. She's always had an eye for a good fellow, my Blanche. You've made no mistakes this time my dear… How delightful! Now this evening's ball can be your betrothal ball as well!'

Blackwood edged his way into the corner, and threw Blanchette and Westbury a bitter look.

Lord Derbyshire came through the door at that point, and came to a halt beside his wife, who was continuing regaling the room with her happiness about Blanche and Henry's announcement.

"I can't imagine anything that could be better – I am so happy for you. Nothing can make today less wonderful!'

'I can think of a few things' said James Blackwood, cynically. He had stepped forward into the conversation as if from nowhere, the ghost at the feast. Everyone present suddenly felt a little muted in their happiness.

'I can think of a few reasons why this wedding should not occur. This couple I fear, have a few tales to tell and no mistake. This whole thing is a sham.' Blanchette felt a sudden hatred for this man prickle within her. What a cad! To try and disrupt their happiness like this and ruin the mood of the day, it was absurd!

And yet she could not but feel deeply anxious at the same time. She had felt sure, just a few hours ago, that he had taken heed of Captain Westbury's words, and would not be a threat to her any more. What if he chose to defy the Captain? Would he tell her father what had taken place between them? Would he rob of her handsome guardsman and her chance of happiness?

To think that she had felt some attraction to this man, and had allowed him to seduce her, nay had even acted to seduce him, in her very own house! She felt a little queasy and had to turn away, as the events of the last few days came rushing back to her. Her feelings must have shown clearly, Blackwood spoke directly to her, bitterness in his tone.

'Now you shrink back, Lady Blanchette – yet you were quite willing to entertain my company this last few days. Quite willing indeed...'

'What are you...' Lord Derbyshire started muttering a confused response, but Westbury stepped in, tall and proud, feigning ignorance.

'To what exactly, are you referring Mr. Blackwood? What is the substance of your allegation?'

Blanche was filled with admiration for him. He had skilfully turned the glare of suspicion onto Blackwood himself.

'Well...' Blackwood stuttered, backing away from the Captain, who was bigger and younger than he. 'I mean, isn't it obvious?'

'Not to me' said Westbury.

'Nor I' said Lord Derbyshire, finding his voice again. 'My dear Blackwood, I should like to know exactly what it is you are referring to here.' Blackwood paused, eyed the room, took in the disapproving, hard faces staring at him. He was not a brave man, when confronted by so many disapproving eyes, and he backed away.

'Oh dash it!' he exclaimed. 'English girls are all just whores and harlots at heart! No good will come of it!' and with that he stormed out, and was not seen in Amfield House, nor heard from by the Cavendish family for quite some time to come.

'Good heavens!' said the Earl, still confused. 'What a remarkable outburst. Do you have any idea to what he is referring?' Blanche and Westbury shared a glance. Charlotte fixed her curious gaze on her sister. Blanche and Henry smiled as one.

'I have absolutely no idea' said Captain Westbury at last, lifting Blanche's hand to his lips and kissing it.

That evening's ball was a glittering affair. The staff had outdone themselves with decorating the room, and preparing a magnificent feast. Flowers filled the huge urns around the room, and a larger orchestra than usual had been persuaded to be available, even on such short notice. Invitations had rapidly been sent to all of the local aristocracy, and many had come to join the house party guests in celebrating Blanche's betrothal.

Blanche had been surrounded by well-wishers from the start, only finding relief when the Captain carried her away from them to dance. Charlotte had watched it all, while dutifully trying, yet again, to hold something approaching a sensible conversation with the young gentlemen who sought her out. Her conversations were as unsuccessful as always, and seeing Blanche so happy made her wonder if she would ever find someone to be happy with, herself.

She had hoped, with all of the extra people in attendance tonight, that there might be some new gentleman to meet, who might, just maybe, be of interest to her. So far, that was not the case. Her mother's mysterious promises of important special guests appeared to be unfulfilled, and generally, of all those present, she seemed to be the only one who was not happy, not having a wonderful time. She was glad that Blanche was happy, but, try as she might, she could not feel happy herself.

Charlotte made her way towards the door, where her parents stood, greeting some late arrivals. She had nearly reached them when a large gentleman bumped her as he passed, and she spent a minute dealing with his profuse apologies, and his insistence on fetching her a glass of ratafia, in apology for his boorish clumsiness. Finally rid of him, she turned and was suddenly arrested in place at the sight of a new arrival - tall, dark, and devilishly handsome.

'Don Diego Sanchez-Zapata' the doorman struggled to say in his Derbyshire accent 'Count of San Pedro, Estanciero of Buenos Aires Province in the Rio de la Plata'. The man nodded approval at the servant's efforts, and surveyed the room, which had fallen silent as everyone gawped at this exotic intruder. An Argentine! Here, at Amfield House? This was most unexpected. Charlotte immediately moved closer to her parents, who were greeting the Don by the door.

'Don Diego!' said her mother, as he kissed her cheek in his sensual, Latin manner. 'We are deeply honoured that you could make it.'

'There is no place that I would rather be on a fine evening in May' he said, in a dark and whispering accent that nevertheless seemed to be used to conversing in English. 'It is so profoundly generous of you to host me, on my return to your fair country.'

'Please, the pleasure is entirely ours! As a bachelor, I am sure you will be pleased to learn that there are many fine young ladies here, who would be more than grateful for the opportunity to converse with an Argentine of your pre-eminent quality! I am sure that they will all be full of questions about your exotic homeland.'

'I am grateful for your generous hospitality. As you know, business compels me to London next week, but for tonight I will be happy to avail myself of your magnificent hospitality.'

'*Mi casa es su casa*, as I believe you Spaniards say!' said her father the Earl, pronouncing the words horribly.

The Don chuckled politely.

'We do indeed, though I regret to inform you, my Lord, your inflexion was a little flat!'

'Ha! Languages were never my strong suit old boy, had to have Cuthbert here look that one up for me as it is!' as the two men were laughing and slapping each other on the back, Charlotte's eyes met those of her mother, who had not realised how close by she was standing. They exchanged a glance, and with a nodding gesture that seemed to say 'would you like me to...' she interrupted the conversation:

'Don Diego, might I present my daughter, Charlotte.' He turned in a single, neat swivelling motion and their eyes met at once.

Up close he was even more handsome than she had anticipated. His face, hardened from riding across the Pampas, yet with soft edges and contours that seemed to invite the viewer in, was immediately compelling.

He had a strong profile with an elegant Roman nose and cheekbones that were high enough to give his face a heart-like shape. His eyes were dark and his skin was the colour of pale liquid caramel. He was dressed in a manner rather exotic for Derbyshire society, with a great red sash running across his navy blue and gold jacket, with its glimmering golden epaulettes. Charlotte could not take her eyes off him, and could almost hear an enticing Latin rhythm playing out in the back of her mind. She knew at once that she must have this man, by any means necessary.

'A pleasure to make your acquaintance, Don Diego' she said, trying to suppress the quaking of her heart.

'The pleasure is entirely mine, Lady Charlotte' he replied, laying a delicate kiss on her hand without breaking eye contact. 'Indeed, it pains me that I have not made your acquaintance sooner. Had I know what an intensely beautiful daughter the Earl of Derbyshire had, I would surely have left Buenos Aires sooner.'

The compliment was delivered with such sincerity and clarity that it was all Charlotte could do to keep her pale English skin from breaking out into a blush. This strange and exotic man had aroused something quite new in her.

'If your mother and father permit it' he added, still holding her in his burning gaze 'it would bring me great joy to share a dance with you.'

Charlotte broke eye contact with the Don for the first time to look over expectantly at her parents. Her father, smiling approval, made a permissive hand gesture. He knew what balls was for, and had enough of an idea of what forces moved the hearts of young ladies.

He was glad to see Charlotte receive some attention, at this point when she had been in Blanche's shadow for so long.

'Of course, Don Diego, I would be very happy to' she said warmly. 'Although, I fear to admit I do not know of any South American dances, having never travelled more widely than England before.'

'Please!' he said, with a steely inner strength. 'There is time enough for both of us to learn more of one another's cultures. I, fortunately, do know some English dances, although I fear that my style is a little more flamboyant than you may be used to. Allow me…' he lifted her hand to his arm with his swarthy hand, and without pondering or apology led her straight to the centre of the dance floor, just as the orchestra began playing a waltz.

Charlotte was both pleased, and nervous, to dance such an intimate dance with the Don as a first dance.

He took her in his arms with much more firmness than any English gentleman, and drew her closer than was seemly. Such closeness only excited her more, so that her heart pounded so loudly she wondered that he did not hear it. His scent invaded her nostrils, and wrapped itself around her – complex and subtle, with something exotic and very un-English about it. She could not identify it – she only knew that she loved it.

Held in a firm pose, she found his approach to dancing already much more passionate than the genteel English dancing going on all around them. They began to move, and it was obvious that the rhythm of the music was something that he connected to, very strongly.

Charlotte was immediately smitten. Feeling the Don holding her close against his lithe body, she could feel her heart hammering even harder, and a great arousal bubbling and boiling up within her. Perhaps this ball was not going to be such a disaster after all. Maybe, for once, others would even envy *her*.

Captain Westbury managed to extricate Blanche from yet another group of well-wishers, and let her towards the dance floor, already anticipating the delicious pleasure of holding her close in the waltz. Blanche was surprised to see her sister, dancing with vigour, and a passion unusual at occasions such as this, with a tall, dark fellow in a strange sort of a uniform, right in the centre of the room. Many of the eyes at the ball were trained fixedly on this rather odd couple, including the prying and suspicious eyes of the chaperones.

Nevertheless, there was little that anyone could do, with the hosts having given consent to this dance, and surely certain allowances could be made for the gentleman obviously being a foreigner. Blanche, still a little giddy from her very intense day, and the joy of her betrothal, was filled with a strange mixture of emotions on seeing this.

A huge part of her was delighted for her sister, who she was well aware was waiting in line behind her, as far as the strictures of the marriage market were concerned.

Nevertheless, despite their sisterly love and affection, she could not but feel a tiny pang of worry on seeing Charlotte in the arms of so handsome a stranger.

As Blanche and Henry stepped onto the floor, joining the swirl of dancers, they looked to where Don Diego was still holding Charlotte close to him as they circled each other dramatically.

'Your sister appears to be quite taken by this Argentine fellow' Westbury commented, clearly amused, like many of the onlookers, by the unrestrained passion of their dancing.

'Yes, I hope that he behaves respectably towards her. I would not want her to be tempted to be as foolish as I was.'

'I am certain that he will be, darling Blanche. For tonight, do not worry – let us just enjoy being together. And let us make sure that your mother plans a fast wedding – I do not think that I could bear to wait very long to have you with me at all times. So much so, that I suspect I may feel the need to sneak into your room very late tonight....'

Her face lit with a brilliant smile at his words, and with that he swept her into the dance, holding her just as close as the Don held Charlotte, letting their betrothal be the excuse for such an intimate hold.

Some hours later, after their betrothal had been formally announced to the room at large, and much of the rather delicious new champagne wine had been consumed, the party, as all parties must eventually, began to die down for the night. First as a trickle, then as a torrent, the guests began to leave the ballroom and retire to their quarters. Almost all were staying at least one night at Amfield House, and might yet stay longer.

There was still food to be eaten, wine, punch, and port to be drunk, conversations to be carried on, hunting for the gentlemen and indoor games for the ladies. And most importantly of all, especially for the young ladies and gentlemen who were here really only for one thing, love affairs to be pursued, and matches to be made.

Many retreated to their beds disappointed by the night's encounters, but many more would struggle to sleep tonight, excited by the promise of passion and future happiness in the arms of a favoured dance partner.

One such sleepless guest, though she was not really a guest at all, this being her own house, in which she had grown up, was Charlotte Cavendish.

She had spent part of the night dancing in a manner and style she had never dreamed possible, and certainly not seen or attempted before, with her Don Diego. In intermittent moments they had stopped to catch their breath and converse, and she had learned much about him. Her fascination with the dashing Argentine had not been dimmed by getting to know more about him - indeed it had been quite further aroused.

So often in her former conversations with young gentlemen, she had been quite bored by their incessant talk of hunting or gambling, of guns and horses and cricket, but here she had found a man who genuinely interested her, and who she was quite happy to simply listen to. He had spoken with such eloquence, even in a language that was not his own, of his country, its great Pampas plains stretching for thousands of miles in every direction, of the Andes Mountains and the Rio de la Plata, of the raw energy and humanity of the city of Buenos Aires.

Charlotte was quite fascinated, and willing to hear about all of his interests. Don Diego was a great reader and thinker, and had many original ideas, especially on the subject of love.

'To feel love, is to be alive' he had said in his beautiful husky voice. He spoke like no Englishman she had ever met, and not merely on account of his accent. 'Whether that love endures and goes on and on, beyond the realm of our physical lives, or whether it burns out, bright and sudden like a candle lit at both ends, this matters not. What matters is to feel, to have that swelling passion within you and to express it with all your heart.'

'Yes, I had never considered it like that, but yes, you must be right.'

'You English, I have a lot of affection for you and your country. I feel you understand this, somewhere deep down inside' their eyes met and it was all she could do not to gasp out her attraction. It rumbled deep within her, anticipating him, penetrating her, from the top of her head to the tingling tips of her toes.

'- and yet I fear you are uncomfortable to express these sorts of things, these sentiments, these, how you say? Emotions. This saddens me. All life is feeling, and love is the prince of feelings.'

As all the other guests were drifting away, to find their beds, or for quiet conversation, including, Charlotte noticed, her sister Blanche, looking exhausted but happy, when they finally decided to end their long conversation and each retire for the night.

At the top of Amfield's grand staircase, beneath the nose of Alfred Cavendish, one of the family's most esteemed ancestors, whose portrait had pride of place, they paused, and Don Diego drew her gently into his embrace. She shivered with delight as he bent his head to place a gentle, sensual kiss on her lips.

Charlotte had never kissed a gentleman before, but immediately felt as if it were all she ever wanted to do henceforth in her life. The Don's lips were sweeter and softer than she had ever imagined human lips to be, and his tongue made swift and skilful motions, playing delicately across her lips, that stimulated a powerful feeling within her, right in her loins. She felt a tingling all over and an urge to cry out with happiness, but then, Don Diego released her, stepping back, retaining her hand only long enough to place a genteel kiss upon it, and turned towards his allocated guest rooms. 'Buenas noches, mi querida' – his soft parting words reached her ears.

Just as he was leaving though, she felt a desperate wish to not let him leave, to have him stay with her, even if only for a few moments longer, and she reached out her hand to stay him a moment, saying:

'Will you be staying with us long, Don Diego?'

'Alas, Lady Charlotte, I must leave early on the morrow, as I have business in London that cannot wait.'

Her heart fell at his words. She had so hoped to spend more time with him!

'I hope, Don Diego, that you will see your way to find the time to visit us again soon. I have found your conversation most... stimulating...'

'Of course Lady Charlotte, I give you my word that I will return to your charming home soon – I could not refuse such a beautiful Lady. You flatter me. But for now, Good night.'

He bowed again and left her, to seek his bed.

Charlotte stood for a moment, watching him walk away, feeling somewhat lost and bereft, then shook herself and set off to her own room, firmly telling herself that she should push aside her fantasies. What could she possibly have to offer such a well-travelled and sophisticated man?

The next morning she felt much improved, and the events of the previous evening seemed like a fantastical dream. The day proceeded with a whirlwind of activities, as her mother set about organising Blanche's wedding.

Captain Westbury had persuaded her parents that he and Blanche should wed with all speed, and her mother had been only too happy to launch immediately into wedding plans.

It was late afternoon when she stood in the entryway, watching Blanche bid farewell to Captain Westbury, who was off for a few days to make his own part of the arrangements. The Captain drew Blanche to him, and, regardless of who was watching, kissed her deeply and passionately. Blanche melted into his arms, and sighed.

'Godspeed Henry – come back to me soon. I fear I am missing you already.'

Everyone laughed at Blanche's words, which she ignored completely.

"Believe me my love, if there was any way to have things arranged without me leaving you at all, then I would never leave!" He bent to kiss her again, then turned for the door. Only to almost collide with a messenger, who had just arrived. Henry bowed, and stepped around the man, striding to his waiting horse.

Blanche stared after him, looking just a little lost.

"Message for Lady Charlotte Cavendish" announced the messenger, looking hopefully at the ladies present. Charlotte, shocked, stepped forward to take the missive from his hand.

'Thank you.'

She never received letters. All her true friends lived close and spoke in person. She wondered who it was from, all the while hoping desperately that she knew. Heart racing, she ignored the curious onlookers, and removed herself to her room. Once inside, Charlotte dared to look at the letter. It was from him! Don Diego's handwriting was as flamboyant as his person, and she could just imagine him sitting down to write it. His exotic scent clung to the paper, and she clutched it to herself for a moment before she gathered the courage to read it.

It was short, but so exciting. He professed his desire to see her again as soon as possible, to spend hours, days, in her fascinating company, and, to that end, he had decided to purchase an estate in England, that he might be nearby. He would see her at Blanche and Henry's wedding, and hoped that she might save more than one dance for him.

Charlotte quivered, her heart bursting with joy! – He wanted to see her, and would soon – the wedding was but two weeks away!

When Henry returned a few days later, and swept Blanche into his arms for a long kiss, Charlotte was no longer envious at all, and was quite certain that she awaited their wedding as fervently as they did.

About the Author

Arietta Richmond has been a compulsive reader and writer all her life. Whilst her reading has covered an enormous range of topics, history has always fascinated her, and historical novels been amongst her favourite reading.

She has written a wide range of work, from business articles and other non-fiction works (published under a pen name) but fiction has always been a major part of her life. Now, her Regency Historical Romance series is finally being released. The Derbyshire set is comprised of 6 shorter novels. She also has a standalone longer novel shortly to be released, and two longer series of novels in development.

She lives in Australia, and when not reading or writing, likes to travel, and to see in person the places where history happened.

To find out first when Arietta's next book is released, sign up for her newsletter at http://www.ariettarichmond.com

Other Books in 'The Derbyshire Set'

(You'll find a taste of Book 3 over the page !)

The Rake's Unlikely Redemption

The Marquess' Scandalous Mistress

Here is your preview of the next book in 'The Derbyshire Set' by Arietta Richmond

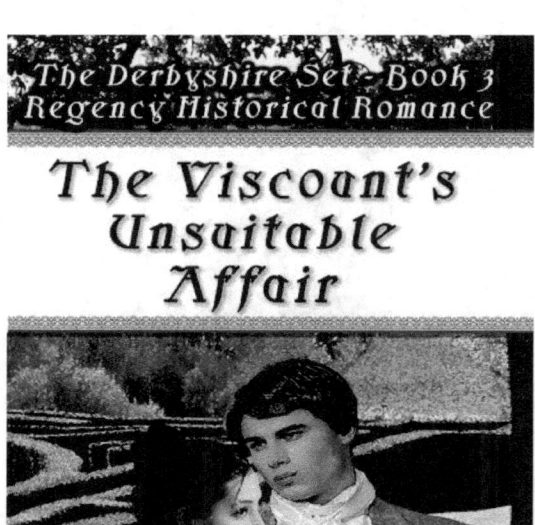

The Derbyshire Set - Book 3

Regency Historical Romance

The Viscounts

Unsuitable Affair

Arietta Richmond

Chapter One

Anna Perkins' hands were shaking along with the jellies on top of the tray. This was the first major occasion since she had been promoted to housemaid, and she desperately wanted to make a good impression. The demands of a huge occasion such as this - the first large house party after the rather scandalous wedding of the houses' master, the Earl of Stanningfield, required input from every single person employed in the household, preparing the feasts and the rounds of drinks or teas that went between, keeping the house neat and orderly without disrupting the guests, and serving everything up in a tidy and efficient operation.

This was how she found herself nervously picking her way along one of the principal corridors of the main part of the house.

A part of it so grand and smart she had barely even seen in her previous role as a scullery maid. She was, despite her protests to the housekeeper and her lack of upper body strength, quaking under the weight of a platter full of jellies.

She rounded a corner and bumped into Richard Maitland. Viscount Bellham. He was striding purposefully away from the rest of the house guests, up this stretch of corridor and walked straight into her. There was nothing she could do. Within a clattering instant, the elegant young nobleman was covered in jelly.

'Good grief!' he was just in the process of saying, making a rudimentary effort to scrape the stuff off his jacket, when their eyes met for the first time. Anna had not had the chance to see many of the guests as yet, and certainly hadn't spoken to any. It had not been her place to look out for handsome young gentlemen, but if it had been, Viscount Bellham would have been the first she noticed.

He was tall and well-built, filling all of the superbly tailored and arranged clothes she had just spilled red and yellow fruit jellies all over. He wore a rich golden waistcoat over a glistening white shirt, with an elaborate cravat, in the manner fashionable in London society, and an elegant dress coat in navy blue. His stance and posture belied an easy confidence, a swagger even. He moved forcefully, as if he always had somewhere important to be, significant things to be getting on with, and would not allow any man, woman or beast to detain him in his endeavours. His breeches clung tight to his well-formed calves and thighs, bringing tight definition to his muscular masculinity.

He had a wild look in his eyes, like a celtic druid or a warrior king, a face encircled by dark, compelling shadows, full red lips and a robust jawline. Atop his head was a beautifully coiffured mane of a rich, golden brown. As she stood beside him, her eyes meeting his, ashamed in an instant of her low status and error with the jellies, Anna felt quite plain in her servants' uniform, and yet he seemed to be peering deep into her soul, communing with her in some profound, impossible way via their two sets of eyes.

His face quickly turned from angry disbelief to soft contemplation of the woman in front of him. She was completely fascinated by this man, whom she knew she could never hope to know more of, than she saw in this instant, and wanted, for some reason that she did not understand, to reveal all of herself to him.

'Richard! What is going on!' the voice came from a young woman, Lady Duckington, one of the few aristocrats present whom Anna had had any contact with.

She had requested, yesterday whilst taking tea in the drawing room, that Anna pick up a handkerchief for her. Anna had obliged, but Lady Duckington had not said even a word of thanks. Anna supposed it was to be expected - most of these upper-class ladies took their own servants entirely for granted, let alone those of other households.

She was a very attractive lady, quite beautiful to look at and extremely well-dressed and well-bred, but she had a coldness of manner that made Anna find her immediately hard to like. Her voice was piercing and harsh, like a January frost.

'Are we going to take this walk in the grounds, or aren't we…' and as she entered the corridor she saw the scene before her. She did not bother to disguise her disgust. Ladies of her station could afford to be disgusted at servants, especially when they were, as Anna seemed to be here, in error. Richard, covered in sweet-smelling slime, turned to face her, breaking eye contact with Anna for the first time in what felt like ages.

'It's quite alright, Lady Duckington' he said in a warm voice that almost glowed with its own attractiveness '- I've merely had a little altercation with a tray of jellies'. Without a second for pause or thought, a rage spread across Lady Duckington's face.

'What in God's name did you think you were doing?!' she exclaimed, partly at Richard, mostly at Anna. 'Idiotic girl! Can you people not even carry jellies correctly?'

'I'm very sorry, my Lady' said Anna, trying to curtsy, blushing with embarrassment, as a sense of desperation rose in her.

'Sorry? You're sorry, are you? Do you have any idea what this gentleman's dress coat cost, or how long the labour of the tailors on Saville Row? I expect you have no idea, but it would be more than thrice your paltry salary! I've a good mind to summon my manservant and have you soundly thrashed in front of us, insolent girl!'

'It's quite alright, my lady' said Richard at last, intervening. He remained calm, even in the face of Lady Duckington's mad fury. Anna, feeling more ashamed and exposed than perhaps she ever had before, was filled with a sudden gratitude towards this man.

Would he speak on her behalf? Was he coming to her defence, her, Anna Perkins, the most junior housemaid at Havisham Hall?

'The fault was entirely mine. I have this unfortunate tendency to not look where I am going in great houses, and to stride around foolishly as if the place is my own. It must come from my father, do not blame this poor girl for my error, it is most unseemly'

'Unseemly?' Lady Duckington all but spat, her fair, round face colouring with her anger, the red of her cheeks clashing horribly with her intricately coiffed golden hair. Anna could not help but think that the Lady brought dishonour to her title by behaving like this and that her fine garments perhaps clothed a character not so fine, but could never have articulated such an insubordinate thought.

'What is truly unseemly Mr. Maitland, is that you, nephew to the Earl of Wiltshire and heir to one of the finest estates in England should have your best clothes drenched in jelly, and then feel a strange desire to speak in defence of a low-born servant! I ask you! You can quite forget about that walk around the grounds! I'm off to seek out the company of someone a little less...' she looked him up and down in disgust. Her face seemed oddly well-used to contorting itself into contemptuous glares '...eccentric'. With that she was off, leaving the two of them alone. Maitland turned to face Anna, smiling, a laugh forming at the back of his throat.

'She isn't always like that' he said, seeing the funny side of the entire situation. 'On occasion she can even be quite charming. On occasion that is...'

'Oh sir!' Anna said, stepping forward in desperation and trying, almost without thinking to soften her country girl's accent in the presence of this prominent gentleman. 'Words cannot express how sorry I am! I thank you kindly for accepting some measure of blame in front of Lady Duckington, but really the fault was all mine, however can I make it up to you?' she realised that in her unguarded moment, compelled by some intense attraction swelling inside her, she had reached out to take one of his hands. Rather than pulling away and chastising her for this completely inappropriate action though, Maitland threw her a dark smile, wry and fascinating.

'Well you can start by ceasing this ridiculous grovelling' he said lightly. She drew back, fearing at once that she had made herself foolish and vulnerable before him.

'- and then when you are quite restored to your senses, you can accompany me to my quarters to help me change into something slightly less...' he sniffed his coat, glistening with the spilled jelly. '- fragrant.' Despite herself, she giggled a little at his remark, and they set off together up the main staircase of Havisham Hall towards the guest suites.

Chapter Two

As befit a man of his status, and his friendship with Charles Rockingham, Earl of Stanningfield and master of this house, Richard Maitland, Viscount Bellham, was staying in one of the finest of Havisham's many chambers. It was, in many ways, a hang-over from Havisham's past, and had not been comprehensively refurbished by the new Earl in a fashionable, modern way, like so much of the front of the house.

A seemingly ancient four-poster bed dominated the room, carved in rich mahogany back in the 16th century and draped in tapestry hangings, that had faded a little with time, but upon which the finely stitched scenes of hunting and feasting were still visible. Only one of the walls had been re-plastered and painted in a light shade, as had much of the rest of the house, to give it a sense of airy lightness, the rest remained wooden panelled, with a heavy, stately air.

There were two landscape paintings facing each other on the west and east walls, an enormous wardrobe and dresser, and the stuffed head of a small deer, shot by the previous Earl, mounted next to the bed. The whole room conveyed a certain antique luxury. Anna did not think she had ever been in this particular room before.

'Ghastly bedchamber really' said Richard as they entered. 'I've no idea why Stanningfield is always so keen to put me up in here, although, I suppose having never complained, I can only really blame myself'.

'The room seems quite wonderful to me sir' she said, still awestruck by its grandeur.

'Yes, I can see why it might, but I can't abide all this old stuff' he replied briskly, tapping at the varnished oak panelling around the walls. 'Don't really like sharing my sleeping space with that old boy, either' he gestured at the deer's head '- but then I suppose it wouldn't be an English country house without some severed animal parts. We of the gentry have a certain image to keep up, don't we?' Anna had no idea what to say in response to all of this upper-class irony. She was gaining insights here that she had never thought she would get, glimpsing a world that had not ever been her own. It was overwhelming and fascinating in equal measure.

'What is your name, girl?' he said, turning to face her again. The fine hairs on her arms lifted, and a jolt of nervous energy ran through her the instant their eyes met. 'I hope I have not bored you into submission with all my talk of great houses?'

'No sir, not a bit'

'Good. Then you won't mind me asking what your name is?'

'Of course not sir, it is Anna Perkins' she said it with a curtsey and practiced look of innocence and modesty. It was good for servants to pretend as if they had no personality at all when they spoke to the upper classes. As far as their employers' were concerned, they were there to fulfil their duty and nothing more. She thought to add, unnecessarily: 'a simple name, for nought but a simple housemaid.'

'Not a bit! It is quite a charming name, in its own way. You need not assume all of us gentle-folk have no interest in our servants as people' he was coming closer to her now. She tried to contain the quivering sensations inside her, as he came so close that she could almost feel his breath mingling with hers. 'We're not all like Lady Amelia Duckington, thank Christ!' he laughed, and she smiled back at him nervously, unsure where she stood.

Softly, gently, his finger stroked her chin, tilting her face closer to his. She was struck by surprise, unsure how to respond to this man, who actually saw her as a person, but at the same time a huge part of her knew that she desired this, desired him. She consented to his touch, allowed him to move her as he wished, enjoying the sensation of his hand on her as he ran his fingers across her skin, silently encouraging it.

'You are a rather fair young lady, Miss Perkins' he said. She instinctively looked away, concealing the redness spreading across her face at this unexpected compliment. 'I am disappointed that I did not have the chance to make your acquaintance sooner.'

Then, in a single movement he turned away from her, and gestured down at his clothes, still covered in the sticky evidence of their earlier run-in. The jelly was already beginning to smell quite strongly, as the heat of his body warmed it through his clothes, thought the practical-minded servant in Anna.

'Come, help me out of these clothes. You cannot deny it; you played some part in their ruin, you can assist me in their salvation.'

'Of course sir!' she said, hurrying over to him at once. He had all but taken his coat off himself, but the jelly had spilled all over the rest of his clothes as well, from his collar, right down to his breeches. Despite her lack of experience with gentleman's clothing, and the fact that she knew that really Viscount Bellham ought to have summoned his valet to perform this duty, and therefore might only have employed her to assist him with some salacious intent, she began at once to undress him. It was most rash of her to do so, but in his presence she seemed to have lost all caution.

Her nimble fingers worked at his cravat, untying the elaborate knot that had no doubt taken quite some time to tie to its perfect, fashionable state, and then easing it away from his neck. She was forced to press herself very close to him to do this, their faces almost touching. The temptation to steal an upwards glance at his face was at one stage too much, but she noted, with more than a hint of disappointment, he was staring imperiously into the middle distance, aloof, clearly used to the attention of servants in this manner.

She then began to loosen the buttons on his waistcoat. The tight definition of the muscles in his chest and abdominal region was clearly visible beneath his well fitted shirt, and she felt a strong desire to run her fingers over the cloth, to feel that hard warm beneath her hand. She resisted the temptation.

The more of his clothes she removed, the more she felt a swelling inside her, a heat rising from her lower body, a desire to feel him, and for him to feel her. It was more than a year now, since John had been killed in the war, and she had not been with a man since, nor wanted to be. Until now. The demands of her position, the need for her to keep at her duties and perform as required, to in no way act above her station, made these sensations all the more acute – how utterly impossible of her, to want a man like this, a Viscount!

Finally, the waistcoat removed, he pulled his shirt over his head and, tossing it carelessly aside for his valet to clean up later, he turned to face her, shirtless, standing tall and proud, awaiting the attention of her hands on his breeches. She took a deep breath, and considered backing out of this situation, fleeing the room, but instead, found herself stepping forward.

'... with sir's permission' she said, as impassively as she could manage.

'Granted, of course' he said, with a grin. She nodded, and began to delicately undo the buttons of his falls, her breathing coming harder s she did so. What would it be like, to run her hands over his hips, to touch his manhood, to bring him to full arousal, to sate her desire with him ?

She pushed the thoughts aside, and focused only on easing down his breeches, over those tempting hips, in such a way as to avoid smearing jelly on his skin. Once the breeches reached his knees, he sat, with care not to spread jelly onto the brocade of the chair, and waited for her to pull of his boots. She did so, with her eyes carefully averted, no matter how much she wished to look, as nothing now preserved his modesty. The boots removed, with a final, faltering pull she slid the breeches from his feet and cast them aside to join the shirt. Turning back she was met immediately with the sight of a throbbing, pulsing manhood, turgid and magnificent. Her nipples hardened, and a pulse of hot need shot between her legs. It had been so long!

Read the rest......

Get

"The Viscount's Unsuitable Affair"

as soon as it's released – go to
http://www.ariettarichmond.com

and make sure that you are signed up for news and release notices !

Other Books from Dreamstone Publishing

Dreamstone publishes books in a wide variety of categories – here are some of our other bestselling books:-

We have books in many categories, ranging from Erotica and Romance to Kids Books, Business Books, Photography, Cook Books, Diaries, Coloring books and much more. New books are released each month.

Be the first to know when our next books are coming out

Be first to get all the news – sign up for our newsletter at

http://www.dreamstonepublishing.com